The Wave

Also by Walter Mosley in Large Print:

Always Outnumbered, Always Outgunned
Black Betty
Devil in a Blue Dress
Gone Fishin'
A Little Yellow Dog
A Red Death
RL's Dream
Walkin' the Dog
White Butterfly
Bad Boy Brawly Brown
Cinnamon Kiss
Fear Itself
Little Scarlet
The Man in My Basement

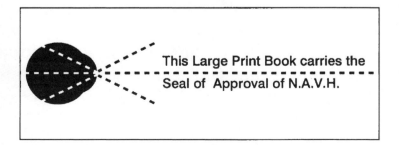

This Large Print Book carries the
Seal of Approval of N.A.V.H.

The Wave

Walter Mosley

Thorndike Press • Waterville, Maine

Published in 2006 by arrangement with Warner Books, Inc.

Thorndike Press® Large Print Core.

The tree indicium is a trademark of Thorndike Press.

The text of this Large Print edition is unabridged.
Other aspects of the book may vary from the original edition.

Set in 16 pt. Plantin by Ramona Watson.

Printed in the United States on permanent paper.

Library of Congress Cataloging-in-Publication Data

Mosley, Walter.
    The wave / by Walter Mosley.
      p. cm. — (Thorndike Press large print core)
    ISBN 0-7862-8398-X (lg. print : hc : alk. paper)
    1. Human-alien encounters — Fiction.   2. Prank
telephone calls — Fiction.   3. National security — Fiction.
4. Large type books.   5. Psychological fiction.   I. Title.
II. Thorndike Press large print core series.
PS3563.O88456W38 2006b
  813'.54—dc22   2005033418

This book is dedicated to
Michael Moorcock,
the Eternal Champion.

As the Founder/CEO of NAVH, the only national health agency solely devoted to those who, although not totally blind, have an eye disease which could lead to serious visual impairment, I am pleased to recognize Thorndike Press* as one of the leading publishers in the large print field.

Founded in 1954 in San Francisco to prepare large print textbooks for partially seeing children, NAVH became the pioneer and standard setting agency in the preparation of large type.

Today, those publishers who meet our standards carry the prestigious "Seal of Approval" indicating high quality large print. We are delighted that Thorndike Press is one of the publishers whose titles meet these standards. We are also pleased to recognize the significant contribution Thorndike Press is making in this important and growing field.

Lorraine H. Marchi, L.H.D.
Founder/CEO
NAVH

* Thorndike Press encompasses the following imprints: Thorndike, Wheeler, Walker and Large Print Press.

1

"... naked, naked ... I don't have any clothes ... so so cold ..."

"Who is this?" I asked.

"So cold," the voice said again.

"Who is this?"

"... cold and naked. Sleeping in the trees."

He hung up then. It was the fourth evening in a week that he'd called. The first night he only grunted and moaned. Two days later, he spoke in single words. Those words were *cold* and *naked*. The voice was definitely masculine but strained and frightened. The next night he used the same two words, but he doubled up on them from time to time, saying, *naked, cold, cold, naked.* He was pleading, but I didn't know what he wanted. He didn't seem threatening, just desperate and crazed.

When I told Nella about it, she said that I should call the police.

"There's no telling what psychotic notions he might have in his head," the buttercream-colored, dreadlock-wearing ceramicist warned. "He might be working up to coming in there and slaughtering you and everybody in your whole house."

"He doesn't even know my name," I said.

"He knows your number," the lovely young Jamaican reasoned.

"He probably dialed it once, and now it's on his redial or something."

"Better be safe," Nella said, "than dead."

I wasn't worried about a few crank calls. In my head, I had worked out that the poor guy was already in a mental institution. That he was on the honor plan or something like that. At night he got confused and hallucinated that he was naked and cold, living in the woods. That's how it was with my grandmother before she died. During the day she was perfectly lucid, talking about old times in Atlanta before she and my grandfather moved to Los Angeles. She had all kinds of great stories about her wild days as a young girl and then, after she was married, about her friends in the church choir. She was also a member of the Southern Christian Leadership Conference.

"Back then Martin Luther King stood down the whole Old Boy system — and

8

beat 'em, too," Grandma Angeline used to say.

Those talks were during the day. But after the sun set, she experienced night terrors. Her husband returned from the grave and blamed her for poisoning him. She would run away from the assisted-living home and wander Pico Boulevard in Los Angeles looking for the bus to Peachtree Street in downtown Atlanta. Sometimes she bullied older male patients in the residence, taking their desserts or pushing them down when their backs were turned. For years the administrators were on the verge of moving my grandmother to a facility that offered more restrictive care.

Then I would go in and talk with her about members of our family whom I'd never met, about whom my father never spoke. There was Albert Trellmore, for instance, the bookkeeper and arsonist. Every Fourth of July, he set fire to one of the big corporations or production companies around Georgia. He loved fires and hated what big businesses did to the poor.

"He burnt lumber companies, banks, loadin' dock warehouses, and big department stores for over twenty-seven years," my Grandma Angeline told me one gray June day. We were sitting on the first floor of the residence, near a glass wall that looked out on Pico. "He woulda kept it up for twenty-seven more if it wasn't for that train-yard fire he set."

"What happened then, Grandma?"

"He didn't think that some'a the hoboes might have been sleepin' under the depot. One of them men died, and it broke Albert's heart. He never set another fire, and died just two years later."

"Why'd he set those fires in the first place?" I asked my eighty-eight-year-old gram.

"White people," she said. "Some of 'em used to refuse to hire black. Some would abuse the ones they had workin' for 'em. Now and then there was a Klansman had all his money wrapped up in one'a them places."

"But why do it on the Fourth of July?"

"Called it his patriotic duty," she said, and we both got a big laugh out of it.

After one of my visits, Grandma Angeline would calm down during the evenings. For a few weeks, we wouldn't get any complaints at all from the residence.

I liked visiting my grandmother. My father, when he was still alive, never wanted to talk about the old days down south. He rarely visited his mother, because she insisted in talking about *all that old shit,* as he used to say.

But I liked her stories, and I didn't care if she went crazy at night and wandered the streets of L.A. looking for Atlanta landmarks.

My mother was from an Orange County WASP family that didn't have many good stories. She cooked the meals and made sure that my sister and I were healthy, but she didn't know how to have fun — at least that's what I thought. And so, when the crazy man who was naked and cold and living in the trees called, I had a soft spot for him like I did for my grandmother and my cousin Albert Trellmore.

That night I dreamed about my father. He was emaciated, as he had been during the last months of his cancer. He had sunken black cheeks and big eyes that seemed to belong to an inquisitive infant rather than a sixty-year-old man. In his last days, he insisted on sitting up and then standing to greet me every morning when I came over to see him. He'd always utter some word that would speak a whole volume in our personal history.

"Kangol," he said on the last morning I saw him.

11

We both loved those hats. Actually, I didn't care much about them, but I wore one because my father had bought it for me.

I made up my mind to go out and buy him a blue Kangol and to bring it as a surprise the next day. I had to go to three different department stores before I found the right one. But when I brought it to my parents' apartment the next morning, they were gone. Their absence could only have meant that my father had died in the night. I sat at the kitchen table until my mother returned. She told me that everything was better now because at least he was no longer in pain.

In the dream, he was just as skinny and still on his deathbed. But he was flexing his muscles and sitting up against a pile of pillows.

"How are you, Dad?"

"Much better, Errol. I'm doing those exercises the nurse gave me. She said if I keep it up, I'll beat this cancer in three months."

An elation spread through me that was so powerful I woke up rising out of the bed. I paced around the onetime garage that was now my home, hoping to find some clue to the dream in my waking world.

2

At three-thirty the phone rang.

"So cold, so very very cold."

"Who are you?" I asked slowly, hoping to calm the poor man's distress.

"Papa," he said. "Papa and, and . . ."

"And what?"

"It's me, Airy," he said, suddenly lucid and almost familiar. "It's me, Papa."

My heart skipped, and I slammed the phone down, catching the nail of my baby finger between the receiver and the cradle. I yelled in pain and knocked the phone over. Then a pall of remorse spread through my chest and into my limbs. I fell to my knees and cried. Soon I was on my belly, racked with sobbing as if my father had died that very moment rather than nine years before. I cried until I had no strength left for crying, and then I fell asleep.

I awoke in a fetal position with the morning light on my face. The sun shone in from a window set in the roof. The phone lay next to me, shattered from the force of my anguish. My baby finger was swollen to twice its normal size, and the nail was black and bloody. With every pulse of my heart, my throbbing hand ached, but all I could think about was the man who called me Airy.

No one but my mother and sister knew that nickname, them and my father. And his voice — it had the right timbre. That was why I had been dreaming of him. The psychotic on the phone not only reminded me of my father, he also sounded like him. Not exactly but similar, down to the way he pronounced my nickname.

I tried to push myself upright, but that sent pain shooting into my finger and up my arm. I finally made it to the bathroom, where I washed away the blood and wrapped the whole hand in an Ace bandage.

The phone gave no dial tone, so I had to walk down to Pico in order to call my doctor from a phone booth. Dr. Singh told me that there was probably nothing he could do about the swelling.

"It will go down in a few days," he said. "No need to come in and pay for a visit."

He knew that I hadn't had health insurance since being laid off as the database administrator for Camcono.com, the online camera and electronics company that had gone belly-up along with so many other online businesses.

"Just keep it wrapped, and soak in warm salt water four or five times a day," Singh said. "I'm sorry, but I must go."

"I told you that you should have called the police," Nella told me when I got to our communal pottery studio that noon.

"What for? He didn't threaten me. All he did was call me by a name my father used to use."

"He called you in your *home*," she said with an odd emphasis on the last word. "That's a violation."

"You sound like he was trying to rape me."

"He's sure enough fucking with your head."

Nella's eyes were a murky brown and green, but they were beautiful. Deep and maybe even a bit primordial. She was the first person I met when I came to Mud Brothers Pottery Studio. She took me under her wing right away, showing me my chores and how to fire the big gas kiln.

"Yeah," I said, "but I feel sorry for him."

"Sorry? You don't even know him."

She was right about that. Still, I did feel

a certain closeness with the voice on the phone. It wasn't my father's voice, but it was similar. I didn't know him, but I felt a kinship.

"So will you call the cops now?"

"Maybe. If you'll have dinner with me."

"I told you already," she said, "I don't date married men."

"We're getting a divorce. You know that. She's living in New York. What more do you want from me?"

Nella smiled then. She stuck out her lips, not so much in a kiss but as an indication that she was considering my request.

"I don't know," she said behind a faint smile. "What would we do on this date?"

"Eat dinner. See a play . . ."

"Hold hands?" She crinkled her freckled brown nose and showed me the space between her front teeth.

"I don't know," I said. "If you want."

"Do I have to kiss you good night?"

"That depends on how much I have to spend," I said. "If it's a cut-rate place on the Santa Monica Pier, or maybe hot dogs from a stand somewhere, then a kiss on the cheek will do. But if I have to dig deep for a play at the Mark Taper Forum, then I'll be expecting some tongue."

Nella's eyes opened wide, and I knew I

had gone too far. But then she squealed and punched me in the arm.

"You're crazy," she said.

Then we went to work.

I had come to Mud Brothers nine months before, after my wife had left me and my job disappeared. I could have gone to work for some big company doing computers, like I had always done, but I didn't have the heart for it. Shelly and I sold the house to a woman named Felicity Fine. I made a separate deal with Felicity so that I could rent the garage for two hundred a month in exchange for light maintenance.

Shelly took 85 percent of the proceeds and then left for New York with Thomas — a far better friend to her than he ever was to me.

I knew how to make cups and bowls, mugs and pitchers from classes I'd taken at UCLA during my undergraduate years. I received free studio time and firing privileges at Mud Brothers for cleaning up every morning and loading and emptying kilns with Nella Bombury.

That day we unloaded the bisque firing from the electric kiln for the children's evening class, and then a glaze load from the big gas-reduction kiln.

I swept. She mopped. I emptied the

trash bins and dusted all the surfaces while she loaded the heavy-duty washing machines in the basement with studio aprons and towels. When I was finished, I went downstairs to help her fold.

At one point we were folding the tarp used by the resident master hand builder. When we came together, Nella grabbed my fingers with hers and brought her face close to mine.

"So where are you going to take me on this date?" she asked in that island-soaked voice.

"A-a-anywhere you want to go."

Later that night she told me it was my stuttering that pinched her heart.

3

I kissed Nella on the lips. We were sitting in my car in front of her apartment building on Adams. She moved her head but didn't open her mouth. We had been to a Caribbean restaurant in Venice and a movie called *The Night Man* at the Third Street Promenade in Santa Monica. We had talked and held hands, and now I was kissing her neck. She made a noise, not exactly a moan, and when I moved my head back, she pressed her hand against my neck, saying wordlessly that she wanted another kiss. I touched her neck lightly with my tongue, and she did moan. I kissed her lips again, but that door was still closed.

I kissed her cheeks and forehead, her eyes and behind her left ear. I came back to her lips, but they wouldn't part. I touched her breast for maybe three seconds before she moved my hand away.

I took the forbidding hand and kissed it. She pushed two fingers into my mouth and pressed down on my tongue lightly. That brought a muffled moan from me.

"What did you say?" Nella asked.

I ran my tongue between her fingers.

"Oooo, baby," she said. "I should bring you upstairs."

I kissed her lips again, and they parted for a long moment. Then she moved back.

"Not so fast, married man."

"She's in New York. We're getting a divorce," I begged.

"No," Nella said. She caressed my cheek with a caring hand. "I just don't want to start out so fast. I only wanted to give you one little kiss, but I didn't know your kisses were so sweet."

She could have pulled my heart right out of my chest. I hadn't been with a woman since Shelly and Thomas hooked up. Shelly and I had been a couple since high school, and she had never once called my kisses sweet.

"Can we wait a little while before we go further?" Nella asked, as if it were really up to me.

When I couldn't come up with the right words, she kissed me lightly, with just a little tongue.

"Okay," I said. "All right. But you know I sure don't want to."

"Wait here," Nella said.

She jumped out of the car and ran

through the door of the large aqua-colored, plaster-faced apartment building. There was a strip of lawn on either side of the front doors and a squat relative of the palm tree to the right. Through the windshield, I could see white clouds passing over, illuminated by a million city lights. The glare of nighttime L.A. was so strong that only a few potent stars were visible. My heart was pounding. The electric air shocked me with each breath.

Where is she? Am I being tested? Should I just leave, or does she want me to sit out here all night waiting for her fancy and her love? Maybe she wants me to go up to her door. Maybe she's waiting for me in a nightgown and here I am sitting in the car like a fool.

These thoughts went through my head again and again. Then Nella came bounding out with a white box the size of a loaf of bread under her arm.

"I'm sorry it took me so long," she said at my window. "But I had it in the closet somewhere."

She shoved the box at me.

"What is it?"

"A phone left over from my last place. I didn't like the way it looked after I painted, so I bought another one."

"Why you giving it to me?"

"Because you said you broke yours, and I want you to call me the minute you get in."

The kiss she gave me through that window was the most passionate I'd ever known. It stayed with me all the way back to my garage-home.

"Errol?" she asked, answering the phone.

"Uh-huh. Who did you expect?"

"Take off your clothes," she replied.

We made love over the phone line, something I had never done before. She was upset when I didn't have coconut oil, but she finally settled for virgin olive. In the beginning, I hardly knew what to say to her. She made me explain every move and sensation, what things felt like and how they appeared. After a while I got the hang of it. She got very excited when I told her to get down on her knees.

It was three o'clock before we said our good-byes. After that, we'd call back every five minutes or so just to make sure that love was still there.

So when the phone rang at ten to four, I answered, "Hey," with certainty that she'd be there kissing my ear.

"Airy, your line's been busy all night."

I knew everything in that moment. Maybe I wasn't sure of how or why or even who, but I knew that my life as I had known it was somehow over. The man on the line was close to me; very much so. My father had used those same words many times after I'd moved out and he'd tried to call. He was never angry, just frustrated and maybe a little frightened.

"Who is this?"

"It's me, Airy — Papa."

"My father's dead."

"It's so cold here, Airy. So cold," he said, as if my reminding him about death brought back the chill.

"Where are you?"

"There's a hut behind the trees. In the woods beyond the graveyard. You can see my stone from here. They leave in the night-time. I sleep on the ground with the sun between the leaves so they don't find me and put me back."

"Who are you?"

"Papa. Papa."

"My father is dead."

"It's so cold, so cold. I sleep in the trees. No clothes."

"Listen, man," I said, my temper running hot with the hormones in my veins. "Who the fuck are you?"

23

"Cold," he said. "Papa . . ." His voice trailed off.

"Hello?"

Maybe ten seconds passed, and then there was a single rapping note, and I knew that he'd put the receiver down on a table.

4

I was at the Fox Hills Memorial Park at seven the next morning. Papa was out there somewhere, just a flat cement disk among thousands. The cemetery director's office was open, but no one was there, so I studied the maps out in front of the building, trying to remember where my father was buried. NY-UEP-CT-1598 was his number. That meant the New Yard in Upper Elysian Park, Circle Terrace, at lot number 1598.

I hadn't been to see Papa in six years. And the graveyard was immense. I had never been there alone. I followed the procession from the chapel the first time, behind the minister we hired to provide the service. My only other visits were with my mother and my sister, Angelique. I never paid attention to which way we were going.

I studied the map for a long time, taking notes and trying to get my bearings by scanning the grounds now and then. Finally I set out to find his stone by myself for the first time since his death.

It took over an hour to locate him.

The New Yard was at the far end of a long curving path that went up a hill and through a section of the graveyard that, as far as I could tell, had no name. I came upon a place called Celestial Gardens, which led me to the New Yard. This was the largest and least expensive area of the cemetery. There were more than a dozen different sections whose names had nothing to do with their placement. There was no Elysian Park or Lower Elysian Park. I wandered through Green Pastures, Holy Rest, and Heavenly Pines before coming upon Upper Elysian Park.

There were five thousand cement disks and more spread out before me. I think it was the immensity of death that brought me to tears again. I hadn't slept at all the night before. In my mind's eye, I'd picture my father, emaciated and dying, one moment and then Nella's smile the next. It's a wonder I found the stone at all.

Arthur Bontemps Porter III
Born
September 19, 1935
Died
January 1, 1996

There was no quote or endearing memorial, just the dates and a name. He never believed in God. He didn't think about death at all. There was no will or life insurance policy, not even a provision for his plot.

"We never liked to think about that kind of thing," my mother said in his defense. "I mean . . . life is so short anyway, why think about dying?"

At forty-nine she had to go to work at the neighborhood newspaper, the *Olympic Gazette*, answering phones, editing articles, interviewing local residents, and even mopping floors for a subsistence salary.

Angelique and I helped her out as much as we could, but now I made very little, and Angie had to watch her money because she was having a baby with her husband, Lon.

The grass around his stone was dirty. I could see the dark soil between the long green blades. I knelt before the grave and pinched the loose soil between my fingers. It was moist and icy cold.

"What you got there?"

I yelped and jumped three paces, spinning around in midair.

I saw the man standing on the concrete

path a few feet from my father's grave, but his features didn't register at first. I didn't know if he was white or black, thin or fat.

"What do you want?" I cried.

"Nothing, son," the man said.

He was wearing gray coveralls, not naked.

"Did he die recently?"

"What?" I asked. "What did you say?"

"Sometimes people come up here years after they lost somebody. Maybe for the first time. It makes the loss feel real."

He was an older man, white. His hair was all gray, and his eyes, I think, were blue. He carried a stick with a nail at the end. Speared on that nail was a Cracker Jack box that someone had carelessly thrown away.

"I'm Errol Porter," I said. "This is my father's grave."

"Fathers," the man said. "It's hard on a son to lose the man who made him. Fathers were once God in a child's eye."

"I miss him," I said.

"I'll leave you, then. Sorry to have disturbed you."

"Wait."

"Yes?"

"What — what's this dirt here in the grass? Is that normal?"

The groundskeeper took a step off the pathway and approached the cut-rate grave. He knelt, as I had done, and touched the soil.

"Rain," he said with certainty.

"It hasn't rained in two weeks," I said.

"But when it does, sometimes the soil comes up. Sometimes it washes down from the parks."

He gestured toward a wooded area not twenty-five feet from the grave. Looking into the thicket of sapling pines, I thought about the woods my late-night caller had claimed to live in.

"Is there a building back there?" I asked.

"Why?" The groundskeeper was suddenly alert, suspicious, even.

"When I came here with my mother, after Dad died, I went off in the woods somewhere to have a cigarette. I remember a small building that had a telephone and a desk."

"Somebody broke in there over the last week. Some bum livin' it up and using the night watchman's phone."

"Wouldn't the night watchman see a man using his phone?" I asked.

"Eric gets spooked out here at night. He spends most of his time down at the main office. He only comes up to make his rounds. We used to have three men at night, but the board of directors got tired of payin' for it. All they got's Eric now, and Eric's a chicken."

"How come there's no soil on the other graves?"

"It pools up in one place or another," the elder man said. "I'm Jacob, Errol. Been workin' at Fox for forty-two years. You want me to clean off your father's plot?"

"I can't afford it," I said. "Lost my job a while back and, well, thanks anyway."

"You're a good boy, Errol," Jacob said, clapping me on the shoulder. "I only hope my own children feel as much love for me when I'm dead and gone."

"I'm sure they will," I said. "I'm sure they will."

5

The borders of the cemetery had high stone and concrete fences protecting the parks. The sides of the walls were embedded with glass and crowned with coiled razor wire. I wore a heavy-duty canvas apron, heavy kiln gloves, and work boots to scale the twelve-foot walls. With these garments, the master builder's canvas tarp, and an aluminum ladder from the pottery studio, I made my way, at two a.m., to the southern edge of the graveyard. That was just off the freeway exit, behind a dense landscape of California pines.

"Are you totally insane?" Nella had asked me.

We were on our four o'clock lunch break. Just before I told her about my plan, we had been kissing in the clay closet.

"I have to go," I said.

"Why?"

"I can't explain it, honey." It was the first endearment I had used with her.

"There must be some reason you got for doing something so crazy."

"It was the way he said that he'd been calling. The way he said the words. The — the inflection," I said, reaching for the right term. "It was exactly, *exactly,* the way my father always complained after I had been on the phone a long time. I mean . . . He could have heard my nickname. He could have looked me up in the phone book and just said Airy because it sounded right. Or — or maybe he once knew an Errol and called him that. But he said exactly the same words, just like my father did. There's no way he could have faked that. Somehow he has to know me or my father. I have to go."

I expected Nella to argue with me, to tell me that I was too crazy to date. But instead she took me home, brought me to her bed, and made love to me as if I were more than twice the man I felt.

At one a.m. I reluctantly left her side.

"Aren't you afraid to go?" she asked me.

"He was my father, Nella," I said. "I know this guy must just be crazy, but I owe him something. His memory, I mean."

An elemental light shone in Nella's bayou-colored eyes. She let her fingers run down my naked thigh, and then kissed my knee.

"At least we'll have this," she said, "before the ghosts out there take you to the Necropolis."

Her words came back to me as I tossed the thick canvas over the razor wire. Nella wasn't afraid that I'd be arrested, but that I'd be captured by the spirits of the dead.

The ladder was eight feet high, and the ground was uneven. I stood on the top rung struggling to maintain balance in my clumsy clothes. When I leaped onto the tarp, the ladder fell over. I had to catch onto the wire through the tarp. And even though I wore thick gloves, one of the razors cut into the ring finger of my right hand. I felt blood in my glove. I kicked and pulled, making it to the top of the wall, buoyed by the fierce coiled wire.

I stopped to catch my breath, feeling safe for the moment. But then the wire shifted and I fell down the inner wall, through a thick network of branches, and to the ground below.

I hit the earth so hard that for a moment all I knew was pain. I pulled off the gloves and held the bleeding finger to stanch the wound and ride out the throbbing ache in my pelvis. As soon as I was able, I got to my feet hoping that nothing was broken. By then I didn't care about the man who said he was my father. All I wanted was to get out of there, to get home to my own bed and to Shelly . . .

I hadn't thought *home to Shelly* in a long time. The air was cold on my neck. My hip hurt, but I could walk. Moonlight winked between the branches and pine needles. I took a deep breath and then stifled a laugh. I had made it over that fearsome wall. Nella's lovemaking came back to me, and I whispered, "Yeah."

I didn't know exactly where I was, but NY-UEP-CT-1598 was somewhere in that part of the cemetery. I clambered up a steep incline through the stand of shrub pine until I came to a plateau of monuments. This was the rich neighborhood, where the wealthy could spread out for their long rest.

There were great statues of angels in alabaster and obsidian that glowed under the three-quarter moon. The caskets were housed in small buildings barred by golden gates. Fresh flowers decorated many of the crypts. Long speeches were etched into stone tablets on almost every burial place.

I limped through the small town of death on a path made from huge, hewn granite plates.

I heard the voice first, before I realized that he was singing. An electric torch shone a little way off to my left.

When a ma-aan loves a woe-man . . .

It must be Eric, I thought, the cowardly night watchman, singing to protect himself from the dead.

He can do her no wrong . . .

I crouched down beside a gated tomb, under the shadow of a great rectangular monolith of black marble. Eric made his way quickly between the vaults, his torch swinging and his voice quavering with fear and love. The last verse I heard him sing — *turn his back on his best friend/If he puts her down* — faded behind a small hill.

I made my way back into the stand of pines to keep from being seen and maybe to find the way to the little hut the crazed hobo had been calling me from.

He attacked me as soon as I was in the landscaped forest, grabbing me from behind and pinning my arms to my sides. I fell to the ground under his weight, thinking that maybe I was going to be murdered. And then I worried that maybe this really was some spirit who intended to drag me down into hell.

6

The man on top of me was naked and foul-smelling. We struggled, but I couldn't exactly call it a fight. He was almost embracing me.

"Airy! Errol! Honey! I'm alive!"

He was skinny, as my father had been in those last months, but this man was young — and strong. He was kissing my face, all elbows and knees, like a child so excited he didn't know whether to laugh or go insane.

I pushed him off. He struggled to get back on top of me, to embrace me, but I pushed him off again.

"Errol," he pleaded.

He got to his feet and held out his hands as if in prayer. The light of the moon illuminated his face. He was a young man, younger than I, and very dark-skinned, as my father had been. He had a mane of matted hair filled with twigs and clods of dirt. His mouth was yowling silently. His eyes were wide with fright and desire.

His penis was uncircumcised, large and ebony, again like my father.

But my father hadn't had a full head of

hair since before I was born. He was nearly sixty-one when he died.

"Errol."

"Who are you?"

"Papa," he said, slapping his chest with both hands.

He went down on his knees and looked up at me. The fear drained from his face, and I could see that this man might well be a younger version of my father. A thought occurred to me. Maybe there was something to what the distressed young man was saying. Maybe he was a messenger from my past.

"Here," I said, stripping off my heavy apron. "Put this on."

His body was rank with human odors. While tying the back strap, I gagged on the smell.

"We have to get out of here," I said.

The grin on his face was that of a penitent's gratitude to a high lord's nod. He ran with me, ahead of me, backward at times — babbling things I couldn't understand because he was laughing while he talked.

We got to the place in the wall where my canvas carpet had been laid.

"We have to climb over somehow," I said. "I had a ladder to get here, but it fell on the other side."

Grinning, the youth calling himself my father scaled the tree whose branches I had fallen through. For a moment I lost sight of him in the boughs. Then I saw him jump a good four feet onto the tarp. He was laughing, and then he was gone. I was sure he'd broken his neck, but what could I do?

I tried to climb the tree, but my cut finger was swollen by then, and my baby finger still hurt, too.

I heard the sound of wrenching metal from the other side and then "Airy!"

The wild man's head had popped up at the top of the wall. He climbed to the middle of the tarp, maintaining his balance in the center. He started moving his hands one after the other in a lifting motion, and the ladder, its brace broken off, appeared over his shoulder and then came down to my side of the wall.

"Climb up, Airy," he called. "Climb up."

I placed the ladder against the wall, making sure the upper rung was secured by the razor wire under the canvas. When I got to the tarp, the maniac helped me keep my balance. Together we lowered one end of the broken ladder down to the outer wall of the graveyard. The young black man clambered down first and then steadied the ladder for me to follow.

It was easy even with my wounded fingers. The experience made me remember times with my father when I was a child. He made things so easy. He'd always been good with his hands. Master carpenters marveled at his work around our home.

"Climb down so good," he said with a wide grin that reminded me of some of the African students I'd known at school. The Africans seemed less guarded, where American blacks kept humor on a lower, more controllable register.

"Who are you?" I asked again.

"Papa," he said with a laugh.

The smell in the car was almost unbearable. I rolled down the window and leaned toward the breeze. I was driving us to my garage apartment. What else could I do? He was a wild man, a madman, but he was surely related to me. I believed that he was some bastard son my father had kept secret. This young man had been reared by a woman, probably a black woman, and somehow he had gone mad craving the affections of his absentee father. Maybe it was like the groundskeeper Jacob had said: this young man had come to his father's grave and lost his mind. Maybe he knew about me from stories his mother had told. Maybe, in his madness, he became that which he so much wanted to have.

He was his own father, and I was this father's son.

"How long have you been out in the cemetery?" I asked.

"Thousands of spans. Twelve thousand nine hundred and fifty-nine and more and more." He giggled and rubbed his palms over the rough apron.

"What were you doing there?"

"Can't count that high," he said, cocking his ear as if to hear a whisper. "Not yet. New numbers falling over, over the line."

"Where were you before you were here?"

"Down, down, down. Down deep and long past. Before the light and the moon and the soft stone crush."

"What's your name?" I asked.

"Good Times," he said with a smile. "Three times good times. Me."

This last syllable came out like a drumbeat. Something about it made me chuckle. Good Times liked to see me smile. He patted me on the shoulder like a demented child petting a dog.

7

My wild half brother screamed when I put him in the shower. The water was warm, but it still tickled him or surprised him. He slipped and fell, tried to get away. But I made him stay and wash all the filth off.

After that I showed him all the places in the bathroom. The toilet and bathtub. The sink.

While I bandaged my cut finger he went around the bathroom touching all that I had shown him, repeating the words as if he were just learning them.

"Rain," he said, pointing to the nozzle jury-rigged above the tub.

"Shower," I said, correcting him, "to get clean."

"Clean," he said. "Pure, perfect . . . the Wave."

"The what?"

"The Wave," he said, smiling brightly. "One after another and then again."

As he said this, he pushed his left palm against his right. At the bottom of the arc, the right hand pushed back and the cycle continued. There seemed to be some truth in what he was doing, something that should mean more to me than I was able to know.

"Clothes," Good Times said.

I had stripped to the waist to wash him. But he was looking at my pants.

In the past few years, I had put on a few extra pounds. There were handles at my sides, and my stomach stuck out a bit. GT (the name I decided to call him) was perfect by comparison. He had almost no body fat, and ropy muscles that flowed easily under his dark skin.

"You can wear my pants," I said, "with one of my belts. Until we can buy you clothes of your own."

GT smiled. He put his hands on my shoulders and looked deeply into my eyes.

"Are you still afraid of the fifty-foot woman?" he asked.

I jerked away from him and fell back against the sink. "How did you know that? How did you know?"

When I was a child, I saw the fifties version of the science fiction classic on TV. I was so frightened that I had to sleep with my parents for three nights afterward.

The smiling youth cocked his head and hunched his shoulders.

Maybe my father had another life some-where, another wife and children whom he told stories about me. It made sense. The only way a young man who resembled my father would know intimate details about my life was if he had known my father, had been told what I loved and feared.

"Are you okay, Airy?"

"What about you, GT? What were you doing in that graveyard?"

"Cold," he said. "Naked."

He shrank back against the wall and slid to the floor. His hands fell down at the sides, and he pressed his knees together. He was the picture of abject defeat.

"Cooooold," he moaned. "Dead."

"Did somebody take you there?" I asked, intent on being reasonable.

"I woke up in a cold sea, on a wave that dragged me down, down, down."

"Was it dark?" I wanted to keep him talking, maybe to pull him out of his bleak reverie with a logic that would release him from the delusions born from his obvious despair over our father's death.

"No," he said. "Bright. Clear. Rippling light forever. And a choir like they had in Atlanta. A choir singing everything ever known. Even me and now you."

"Me?"

GT was smiling now, sitting with his back straight against the wall.

"Yes, you, Errol. Because I know you, and you are in my heart. And so now the whole earth sings about you on the edge of a Wave that goes around and around forever."

He was a grinning fool on the floor, his hands held out in a Christlike gesture.

"Where were you born?" I asked him, and he looked at me as if I were the fool.

I got him to put on a pair of my jeans and a black T-shirt decorated with a picture of Mao Tse-tung delicately etched in gray and white across the chest.

I took out a family album that Mother had made for me and my sister on the first anniversary of Dad's death.

"That's my father," I said, pointing at a picture of him taken when I was thirteen. We were at a Little League game in Pomona. I spent most of the time on the bench, but he was still proud that I had made the team.

"I remember that day," he said. "You got sick in the car on the way over. You were so nervous."

Another detail my father could have told him, I assured myself.

I turned the page. There was a picture of my mother in her wedding gown, surrounded by a group of white and black women. She was striking and quite young, smiling brightly and standing erect.

"I can't look at this!" GT shouted.

He pushed the book to the floor and scrambled off the couch. He fell but bounced up quickly. Tears were streaming from his eyes. He looked even more wretched than he had in the bathroom.

"It's so sad," he whimpered.

"What?" I asked.

"Death. Dying. Lonely creatures forlorn in the twilight, the half-life, the sad sad waiting and hungering and longing for a memory."

"I don't understand. Are you talking about my mother?"

"She never really loved me, Airy," he said.

"She never knew you, GT."

"She loved a man called Bobby Bliss. He had a house on Myrtle Street. She told me that she loved him. That's what she said."

He seemed to calm down after saying these words. He made the circular gesture with his hands again and then smiled.

"But all of that is over now. Kingdom

has come." He smiled at me with that African grin.

"It's time to go to bed," I said. "You can have the couch over there. I'll get you some blankets."

He followed me to the trunk next to my bed, on the other side of the large room. I took out the blankets my mother had given me when she found out that I was living in the drafty garage. I handed these to him and then began to undress.

The deranged young man watched me strip down to my boxers. He started taking off his own clothes.

"You go to the couch, GT," I said.

"Can't I sleep with you?"

"Men don't sleep together."

"You slept in my arms for three nights after dreaming that the fifty-foot woman was after you." Again he sounded just like my father. The inflections, the insinuation, the hint of Atlanta hovering between his words.

"No, GT."

"But I'm scared, Airy. Scared of the dark and the cold."

A tear rolled down his cheek.

It was a big bed. Shelly and I had bought it together at an antique store in Venice. She had spent long afternoons with Thomas, the onetime captain of our high school football team, in that bed. Sometimes I wanted to burn it. But I needed a place to sleep.

"No funny stuff," I said to GT.

He grinned and jumped on the mattress like a small child, giggling and pulling the covers up to his chin.

I turned off the lights around the garage and then climbed in on the other side.

"Good night, Airy," GT said happily.

"Good night."

"Airy?"

"Yeah?"

"The whole world is sleeping, but soon it will be morning. We will all rise up and be remembered."

There was a song and a broad field of light gently undulating, ululating, rising higher with each swell and cry. It was cold and burning hot, but neither temperature bothered me. There was a firmament of ice so clear that I could see for miles through it. Deep within the ice were flames echoing the sun. Every breath I took was the first breath on a perfect summer's morning. And there was no place but many places all at once, a jumble in my mind.

My mind was the jumble, however, not

the places. They were set on a sea of awareness that knew only numbers, but numbers were everything.

I started screaming at some moment, and the numbers switched register. Hot became cold, and the clear distance became opaque; it never ended, never changed for a billion trillion beats and then again.

8

GT was hugging me from behind, but I didn't feel sweaty, as I had when sleeping so closely with Shelly. When I realized that he had his arm slung over my shoulder, I pushed him away.

"I told you, no funny stuff," I said.

"You were screaming in your sleep," he explained. "When I put my arm around you, you calmed down like you used to when you were a little boy and afraid of what was in the cabinet under the sink."

Could my father have told GT's family so much about me while we never even knew that they existed? Everything about the young man unsettled me. His voice and his knowledge about me, his lunacy. It was all crazy, like a bad dream I couldn't awaken from or a daydream I couldn't shake.

"Is something wrong, Airy?"

"Go take a shower, GT," I said. "Take a shower and let me get my head together."

He bounded out of bed and went to the makeshift bathroom.

Watching him go, I thought about my father. Even if he'd had another family some-where, he had still been a better man than I. I had no money and no children. My wife was divorcing me for a man who, she said, "was better than you would be on the best day of your life."

The phone rang.

"Hello?"

"Well?" Nella Bombury said in my ear.

"It's a little hard to explain," I said, lifting the bandage to inspect the deep cut in my ring finger.

"Did you go?"

"Yeah."

"And?"

"He's here."

"What? You brought a zombie home from the graveyard?"

"He's not a zombie. Just a kid. Con-fused, you know."

"And you slept with him in your house?"

"He'd been living in a graveyard," I said by way of explanation.

"I'm coming right over." Nella hung up on me.

Nella wasn't even quite my girlfriend, but she was running to my side to protect me. Shelly had never done anything like that. She never worried about my safety or well-being. I was her boyfriend, then her husband, but at our ten-year high school reunion, she met her man — Thomas Willens.

We'd been friends in high school, Tommy and I. He was an amiable sort, never frowning or worried, like me. I remember he used to say to me, "Aw, come on, Flynn, what could be so bad?"

I went to my computer and signed on to my ISP. I looked up cemeteries in Southern California inside of news items. I wondered if there had been strange activities reported from other southland graveyards. There was nothing of interest. The usual desecration stuff. But no movement to take on the identities of the dead.

Hi, Errol.

The words popped up on my screen. The sender was Shellyshell11.

I didn't answer.

I saw that you were online and I thought I'd see how you were doing. I'm at our place in Chelsea. It's really hot in New York.

Our place was what I focused on. Shelly and Thomas making a home for themselves.

"Look at me!"

I turned from the screen to see that GT had wrapped himself into three blue bath towels. One for his waist, one for his shoulders and one for his head. He was grinning and strutting in the ensemble.

"I made my clothes, Airy. I dressed myself with just this fabric I found."

"You need pants and a shirt to go outside."

"Why?"

"Because people don't count towels as clothes on the street."

He pouted and sat on one of my kitchen chairs.

I had separated the garage space into different areas. The center was my living room, marked off by a table, two chairs, and a couch. In the four corners I had my bedroom, kitchen, office, and bathroom. The bathroom was the only space around which I had erected plasterboard walls.

"I like it," GT complained.

"Me too, man. But if you go outside like that, they'll arrest you."

"Arrest," he repeated, playing with the word, moving it around. "Rest. Cell. Restrict. Like death. Death."

"Where were you born, GT?"

" 'lanta."

"Is that where your mother is?" I remembered that my father had made a few business trips to Georgia when I was a boy. Maybe that was when he would visit his second family.

"She's in the graveyard I rose from."

"Not my grandmother," I said. "*Your* mother."

"I am Arthur Porter, Errol. I'm your father. At least I was. Now I'm your father and part of the Wave."

"What's the Wave?"

"Move-ment," he said, making the circular motion with his hands again. "Motion."

"It's a movement? Like a cult?"

"It is the whole world. Living planet. The one and the many." He closed his eyes, and ecstasy crossed his face. "Every beat and count remembered and passed on."

"Are you're a member of this group?" I asked, trying to get past the spiritual hocus-pocus.

"Yes," he said, smiling brightly, his eyes still closed.

"Do you have a title?"

"I am a memory of the ancestors of the numberless. I am rec . . . reco . . . recollection. Recollection, yes."

The knock on the door didn't faze GT. I

left him smiling at the deep elation brought out by his gibberish.

Nella was at the door, wearing a yellow sundress with a wide-brimmed red straw hat. There was a cloth bag slung across her shoulder, and on her feet she wore blue wooden shoes. My heart skipped at the thought that such a wild and beautiful woman could be my lover.

"Where is it?" she asked.

"He's on the couch. Don't scare him, okay?"

She moved past me, clacking her wooden heels on the concrete floor. She walked right up to GT, who was still in his blind reverie. He opened his eyes when her shadow fell across his face. His smile was beatific.

"What are you?" she asked him.

"A memory."

"A memory of what?"

"Of who I was. Of all those that I knew. Of the move-ment under the earth. Up from the deep, our destiny."

"Are you from hell, then?" Nella asked.

"I came from hell," he said. "But that was before I was put in the ground. That was your world. Yours and Airy's."

"Take that towel from your head," she commanded.

GT did as she told him. He threw off the towel, revealing his matted mane.

She searched through the hair with her fingers, rubbing his scalp and pulling on his locks.

"You don't have horns," she said at last.

"Are you my son's lover?"

"All right," she replied.

"You are very beautiful. Eyes and skin, teeth and bone. Do you love him?"

"I . . ." She hesitated, staring deep into his eyes. "Did you climb out of the grave, Mr. Porter?"

"Yes. I rose from the deep memory, replenished by the numberless, reminded, readied, and then released."

Nella sat down next to the wild-eyed youth. She took his hands in hers and examined his fingernails. They looked perfect, from where I stood.

"Did you claw your way out?"

"I flowed through the mud. First one cell, then the second, then the first again. Like leapfrog. Leapfrog." He grinned madly.

"And when did you come awake?" she asked.

"You don't believe this shit, do you?" I asked Nella, interrupting the spell.

"I just want to hear what he has to say for himself," she said.

"There's nothing to know. He's crazy."

"No, Airy," GT said while keeping his eyes on Nella. "I am a syllable in the annunciation. The word echoed back into the air."

"No, GT. You're a kid. You're confused. That's all."

"Then why did you bring me to your home? Why did you let me sleep in your bed?"

"You slept with him?" Nella asked.

"He was frightened."

"And so you put him in your bed?" she asked. "Did you take off your clothes?"

"Make up your mind, Nella. Either you think he's a zombie or my gay lover."

"He might be both."

"And my father, too?"

This last argument seemed to stump her, at least for the moment.

"He's just some crazy kid, probably a relative, who believes he's become my father. I think he might be a half brother from some other family. Probably from Georgia."

"Why you say that?" she asked.

"He looks a little like my father. Around the eyes and cheeks."

"Do you have a picture of your dad when he was a young man?"

"No. My sister has those pictures."

"Let's go look at them."

"Why?"

"Let's just go," she said.

I liked her fiery side, her quick decisions. I needed to be led. Since my wife left and my job evaporated, I couldn't seem to get going. The only reason I continued to work at the pottery studio was because Nella always urged me on. Some days, when I didn't show up, she'd call to make sure I was going to come in and work on my line of mugs.

"Get dressed," Nella said to GT.

When he shed his towels, a gasp of appreciation escaped my new girlfriend's lips.

"My," she said, "they didn't leave anything out when they resurrected you."

9

"The wind," GT sang in ecstasy. "On my face and down my skin. The wind is the greatest joy in the wide world."

He was again wearing my jeans and the Mao T-shirt. His head and shoulders were thrust out the window of my Civic. I had owned that copper-colored car since before my marriage.

"Get back in the car, GT."

"But it's so beautiful, Airy. It's so fast."

". . . in other late-breaking news," the radio announcer was saying, "a deranged man pushed two police officers from a three-story roof in downtown L.A., seriously injuring both men. The officers were responding to the complaint that a vicious dog had been threatening nearby residents. The man, possibly the owner of the dog, fled with the animal when police arrived. They chased him to the roof of the downtown apartment building and were surprised by the man. The attacker eluded custody, and an intense search is now being conducted in a ten-square-block area . . ."

"Get your head back in the car before someone knocks it off, fool," Nella said to GT.

In response, GT pulled his head in, took off his T-shirt, and then shoved most of his upper torso back out the window.

"The wind!" he shouted.

While Nella shouted at GT, the radio announcer was saying something else about the man and dog running from the police. I was looking for my sister's street, which was off Olympic and east of La Brea.

"Pull over," an amplified voice commanded.

At first I thought it might have been the radio, some kind of joke that the announcer was making about the runaway felon. But then I looked in the rearview mirror. Blue and red lights were flashing. The police car pulled up on the driver's side.

"GT!" I shouted. "Get the fuck back in the car."

He jumped to obey while I pulled to the curb.

"Oh shit," Nella said.

"What's wrong, Airy?" GT asked sheepishly.

"Just be quiet," I told him. "Stay still and don't talk crazy."

"Okay."

In the mirror, I could see the policemen coming up on either side of the car. One white and the other black, they both had their hands on their guns.

"Please step out of the car," the black officer, the one on my side, said.

GT and Nella got out of the passenger's side. We all moved toward the curb, while passing cars and pedestrians slowed to gawk at us.

"Let's see some I.D.," the black officer said.

He wasn't really black. He had dull gold-colored skin with dozens of dark freckles in groups around his face.

The white cop stood three or four paces away with his palm on the butt of his revolver.

Nella and I took out our licenses.

All GT had was the T-shirt wadded up in his fist.

"What about you?" the black cop asked GT.

"That's my cousin, Officer," I said. "He's had some emotional problems since the death of his father."

"What's your name?" the cop asked, still addressing GT.

"Arthur Bontemps Porter, Officer."

"Why were you hanging out of the window like that?"

While the black cop interrogated GT, the other one moved to look in the windows of my car.

"I was homeless for a while, sir," GT said. "Airy took me in. I guess I was a little, um, uh, overjoyed."

The change in the young man was nearly complete. None of the mindless exuberance showed in his demeanor. His eyes still lacked concentration, but the light of insanity was almost completely extinguished.

"Walk over to that fire hydrant and back," the cop said.

GT did so. The only problem he had was that he was wearing a pair of my old tennis shoes, which were a size or so too big. His walk was a bit sloppy, but he moved in a straight line, as far as I could tell.

"Touch your nose with the point finger of your left hand," the policeman commanded.

GT complied.

"Now your right."

The mad youth was as obedient as Beefeater.

"He's your cousin?" the cop asked me.

"Yes, sir."

"And who are you?"

"Nella Bombury," Nella said. "I'm Errol's girlfriend."

"What's wrong with you?" the cop asked, looking directly into GT's eyes.

"I just got out, Officer. I was in a — a crazy place, but then they put me back together and let me out, and — and after a while, I called Airy and he took me in. Him and his girl."

"Where's your identification?"

"I hold on to it," I said then. "GT loses everything. I'm sorry, but I didn't think to bring it along today. You see, we're just going to my sister's house, and so I didn't think we'd be needing it."

"Where does your sister live?"

"Two blocks up," I said. "On Croft."

"It's very dangerous to allow a passenger to lean out of the window when the vehicle is in motion, Mr. Porter," the policeman said.

"I'm sorry, Officer. I won't let it happen again. I promise."

"And get him some clothes that fit," the man inside the uniform suggested. "If his clothes fit, then maybe he'll feel more normal."

"Yes, sir."

Angelique was seven and a half months into a difficult pregnancy. The simple effort of answering the door exhausted her.

"Hi, Errol," she said wanly, looking at Nella and then GT. "What are you doing here?"

"Can we come in, Angie?"

"Oh." She hesitated. "I guess so."

Angelique and Lon lived on the ground floor of a three-story house that had been subdivided into three apartments. Light flooded in from every window. The floor was bright pine, and all of the furniture was lightly varnished white ash. Lon was a carpenter and a furniture maker. He was from a South Carolinian ex-slaveholding family that had broken off contact with him when he married my light-skinned sister.

I was the darker of the two children. Angie looked almost white. But Lon's parents wouldn't have cared if she'd been blond and blue-eyed. Black was black, where they came from. I guess that was why Lon moved to L.A.

Angelique sat us in the living room. By then she was stealing concerned glances at GT.

"This is Nella Bombury, Angie," I said as soon as we were seated, "my, um . . . And this is GT."

"Hi, Anj," GT said. "How's the Waterwog?"

The shock registering on my sister's face brought me all the way back to our childhood. Her wide eyes gawked, and her jaw dropped down as if there weren't a bone in it.

"Daddy?"

"Baby girl," GT said.

He went to sit by her and folded her in his arms.

Nella looked over at me with *I told you so* radiating from her face.

"No," I said. "He's a fake, a sham. He is not our father."

10

Angelique accepted GT as her father with no qualms and few questions. I thought at the time that it had something to do with her pregnancy; the life growing inside her enhancing her spiritual side.

". . . and do you remember when we went down near Pismo Beach that year there was that big windstorm . . ." my sister was saying.

". . . and Airy held out his coattails like wings, and the wind caught him and he went flying over the edge," GT said, finishing the sentence, further proving to my sister that he was our father come back from the dead.

"Mama was so scared," Angelique said.

"But," GT continued, "he landed in that scrub oak just over the drop and cried for all he was worth."

I didn't remember the event because I'd been too young. I doubted if Angelique did, either, but our parents had told the story so often that she believed she was calling on her own memory.

"It's just a story," I said. "Somebody, probably our father, told GT when he was a child. Now he thinks that he was there, but it's just the same as you, Angie — you've heard it so often that you think you remember me falling. But you don't."

"I do," she said.

"She might remember, Errol," Nella said. "How do you know what's in somebody else's mind?"

"Because I was five when it happened, and she was only three."

"Three-year-olds can remember," Nella argued.

"But I don't even remember," I said.

"You're the one who fell," she reasoned. "Maybe it was too upsetting. Maybe you blocked it out."

"Look at him. He's not even twenty. How the hell could he be our father?"

"Here," Angelique said.

While Nella and I argued, my sister had gone and gotten the family album our mother had made for her. She opened it to an old black-and-white photograph of Dad. He was sitting in a chair set before a fake backdrop of a potted fern and a window looking out onto a large painting of an empty beach. He was smiling, with

66

his legs crossed, wearing a light jacket and dark trousers.

He was the exact duplicate of the man sitting on the couch before me.

"GT's probably his son," I said again. "That's the only explanation. Dad had a second family, one that he never told us about. You know how he loved to tell stories. He probably sat around with GT here and told him about us, about the big stories. I'm sure there are some things he couldn't know."

GT was smiling at me. He had one arm around my sister and his bare feet out of my shoes and crossed before him. I had seen my father sit like that a thousand times in our old house, on the old sofa.

"What are you grinning at?" I asked the young man.

"You were always stubborn, Errol. Always trying to prove something in your mind when the truth was right before your very eyes."

"You can't be who you think you are, GT," I said. "My father is dead. He died nine years ago. How could you be him?"

"I'm not him," he said, "not exactly. I am his memories, his blueprint. His heart."

"How can that be?"

"The Wave."

"What's that?" Angelique asked.

"Some cult he belongs to," I said.

"It is the fount, Waterwog."

"Where we all come from?" she asked, bedazzled.

"Yes," he said. "And where we all shall go."

"This is crazy," I said. "He was a homeless man living in the graveyard until yesterday. How can you think he's some kind of second coming?"

"Why not?" Nella and Angelique said together.

"Because," I said. "Because it doesn't make any sense. People don't just rise up out of the grave."

"Jesus did," Nella said.

"My father wasn't any kind of Jesus. He didn't go to church. We had to pay the minister to read over his grave because Dad had never been inside a church."

"I know," Angelique said. "Let's ask Mama."

"We can't do that."

"Why not?"

"Because what if he isn't some divine spirit and instead the nutso bastard son of our father who is still dead? How do you think Mom will feel about that?"

"We could call her up and ask her a

question that only she and Papa would know the answer to. Something that he'd never talk about to children."

"She has a strawberry tattoo under her left breast," GT said.

"What?" I asked him.

"She has a strawberry tattoo under her left breast," he said again. "Bobby Bliss made her get it. She said that she just went crazy one day, that her hairdresser told her about a tattoo parlor. She said that all the girls from the beauty shop went in to get them, but later on, she admitted that it was her lover who wanted her to make the vow to prove she loved him."

Tears flowed from GT's eyes again.

"Mama cheated on you?" Angelique asked.

"She said that she still loved me as a friend, but her heart belonged to him. We stayed together because of you children, but our bed was cold as a stone."

I thought about Shelly and Thomas Willens, about her coming in late every Tuesday and Wednesday for six months. She'd said that she had a flower arranging workshop, that they all went out for drinks after the class. To prove it, she brought home samples of flowers that she had arranged.

Fool that I was, I believed her.

"Newspaper," she said, as she always did when she answered the phone at work.

"Hi, Mom, it's me," I said.

"Oh, hi, Errol. I was just thinking about you. Are you all right?"

"Sure I am, Mom. I'm fine. How are you?"

Angelique wasn't exhausted anymore. She'd made tea for Nella and was holding GT's hand. They were all sitting on the blue couch, the one soft spot in the blond-wood room, watching me talk on the cordless phone.

"I'm fine, hon," my mother was saying. "Have you gotten a job yet?"

"I've made a line of mugs, Mom. I'm going to be selling them at the Third Street Fair in Santa Monica."

"That's nice, honey. But have you at least called AT&T? Mona Ramp says that they've been hiring computer people."

"Uh-huh," I said. "Yeah, you told me. Listen, Mom. I have something to ask you."

"What is it?"

I spied a huge white cloud out Angie's window. It seemed to be rearing up like a great reptile, but not a species I had ever seen before.

"I'm here at Angie's house," I said, stalling.

"Oh. How is she? I hope you're not making her serve you, Errol. You know she's having a hard pregnancy. I had the same problems when I was carrying you."

"Do you have a tattoo, Mom?"

She made a gasping sound and then was quiet.

"Mom? Mom?"

"Why would you ask me something like that, Errol?" It was as if there were a different person on the line. Not my mother at all. Or maybe she was my mother, but the tone of her voice said that I was the stranger, the threat.

"Do you?" I asked, driving the wedge deeper between us.

"I don't know what you're talking about." If I hadn't been her son, she would have slammed the phone down, I was sure of that.

"A strawberry tattoo," I said. "On your — your chest."

"Oh my God. Who have you been talking to? What have they said?"

11

My mother lived in the upper half of a du-plex, set behind another duplex on Raleigh, near Santa Monica Boulevard. She asked me to meet her there in an hour, and I agreed.

The apartment had been too large even when she and my father lived there alone. Now she might as well have been living in a warehouse. There were four beds in as many bedrooms, dozens of chairs, four tables, and three television sets. The apartment had ten rooms, not including the two and a half baths and kitchen.

Despite the large apartment my mother was a small woman. She could have lived in a studio. She was only five feet tall, and slender, with short gray hair and big gray eyes. She hadn't been beautiful at any time in her life, but the intensity of those eyes made up for it. Her love exhibited itself as anxiety instead of warmth. She had wor-ried about me and Angelique, making sure we were healthy and clean and getting along well at school.

She answered the door, looking past me.

"Did Angelique come with you?" she asked without greeting.

"Can I come in, Mom?" I said.

"Of course you can, honey." She backed away from the door, looking me up and down.

"You've put on a few pounds," she said.

"Yeah. You got some coffee?"

The TV in the den was on. The TV was always on in there, usually set on one of the news channels. I didn't ask her to turn it off. The set had been on pretty much nonstop since the day my father died.

"It keeps me company," my mother had complained when Angie and I asked to shut it off. "If I get up in the middle of the night, it's here waiting for me," she added. "The light keeps me from tripping and falling down."

The national news was on, but the volume was pretty low. She served me coffee in my favorite mug, with just the right amount of half-and-half.

"Who told you about that tattoo?" she asked as I took my first sip.

"A guy I met in the cemetery."

"What?"

I told her the whole story. From the late-

73

night calls to breaking into the graveyard and bringing GT home. I told her about his delusions, too.

"Where is he now?" she asked. Her words were stiff, I think because she agreed with me in thinking that GT was probably my father's bastard son.

"So did you have an affair, Mom?"

"It was all a long time ago, Errol," she said. "We all make mistakes."

"So you had an affair with a man named Bobby Bliss?"

My saying the name horrified her.

"He told you his name?"

"Yes. He knew that you were with him."

"But I never told him Bobby's name," my mother said. "I never told him that. He said Bobby Bliss? You're sure?"

"I don't know what to tell you, Mom. He knew your boyfriend's name. I figure it's because Dad used his second family to say things that he couldn't say here with us."

"He told you about the strawberry tattoo?"

"Yes."

"And about Bobby?"

"Yes."

"Where is this young man now, Errol?"

"He's at Lonnigan's diner with Angie and my friend Nella."

"Okay," she said. "Finish your coffee, and then let's go talk to him."

Lonnigan's was a throwback to the coffee shops of L.A. in the eighties. It was red and glass with a roof shaped like an artist's palette set on a tilt. There was a long chrome counter and booths in the windows. Nella and Angelique were sitting at a large booth with the handsome, wild-maned young man when my mother and I arrived.

On the ride over, she'd sat silent. That silence was the mark of her anger. Her hands were in her lap, and every now and then she'd take in a deep breath through her nose. She was wearing a simple gray button-up dress that came down to around her shins.

She walked with a quick step to the door of the restaurant and then steadily toward the booth.

But when she got close enough to get a good look at GT, she fell backward into me.

"Oh my God."

GT stood up, all smiles and welcome.

"Hey, Sprout," he said in just the tone my father had used every morning. "How's the little Sprouts?"

"Artie?"

My head felt like it was going to break open. If he could fool my mother, too, then maybe my newfound half brother really was my father. I mean, if enough people believed it, why couldn't it be true?

"How have you been, Madeline?" GT asked.

He reached for her hands, but she pulled away.

"You're not Artie," she said.

Relief flowed through me.

"You can't be," my mother continued. "But how do you know all of those things you've been telling my children?"

"Come and sit, Maddie," he said. "Let's talk about it. Let's talk."

The craziness had subsided again. He moved differently. His tone was reasonable. I noticed that the T-shirt was tucked into his pants.

We all sat.

"Mom, this is Nella," I said. "She's my friend from the pottery studio."

"Pleased to meet you," my mother said without even a glance at my new girlfriend. "Now, answer me, young man. How did you know the name Bobby Bliss?"

GT laced his fingers together and leaned forward. He smiled and shook his head slightly.

"So it's true, Mother?" Angelique said. "You did cheat on Daddy."

"Be quiet for a minute, honey," our mother said, the way she used to when we were small children. She kept her gaze on GT's face. "You can't be Artie, you know."

"Why do you say that, Maddie?"

"Because Artie had a scar below his right eye. He got it roughhousing with another boy when they were only nine."

All right! Finally some proof, I thought.

"I already told Airy," GT said, "that I'm not exactly Arthur Porter but the memory of him made flesh."

"Then what about the scar?" I asked.

"The memory doesn't include physical pain," he said, and then he looked at my mother. "Only the pain of the heart and mind remain."

"Are you his son?" my mother asked.

"In one way," GT said. "I have learned from his mistakes. And, of course, I've entered the Wave."

"How dare you tell my children about these things?" my mother asked the now strangely mature youth. "You have no right."

" 'When I think of you,' " GT said, obviously quoting from something, " 'my breasts surge against my clothes, my feet get restless and the touch of my plain cotton skirt takes on an intimacy that the most ardent lover could never know —' "

"Stop it," my mother said. "Artie never knew Bobby Bliss's name. How could you? I mean, you're no more than twenty. Bobby went away before you were born."

GT's smile faded then. His fingers unlaced, and he looked down at his hands.

"I hired a detective," he said, then he shuddered. "He followed you" — another shudder — "and took pictures. It was after you told me about being in love with another man, Sprout."

"No," she said.

My sister was crying softly as Nella shook her head in disbelief.

"You see, Errol," GT said, "I confronted your mother when I began to suspect. She told me that she was in love with another man, but she wouldn't say who it was. She told the real story of the tattoo and promised never to see him again. But she lied." He looked at her, and she looked away. "I hired the detective, and he brought me proof."

"Did Artie make Bobby break it off with me?"

"Yeah," GT said. "Yes, I did."

In that instant GT took on the demeanor of an old and broken man. He could have been my father, almost.

We were all silent for a while after that. Angelique and I were trying to comprehend the deep drama that had unfolded while we were going to school and living blissfully, blindly ignorant. GT was lost in sorrow. I have no idea what my mother and Nella were thinking.

After a long while I said, "That still doesn't prove anything. My dad could have told you or your mother all of that. It doesn't make you our father."

GT shuddered again, this time so violently that he fell from his seat to the floor under the table. I pulled him out from the booth, but he stayed on the floor, shaking and groaning.

"What's wrong with him?" a waitress asked from behind the counter. You could see the fear in her eyes.

"It's an epileptic fit," I said, and then I made a decision.

"Nella, help me get him out to the car," I said.

I got my shoulder under his arm and dragged him toward the door before she could move to help me.

"What are you doing?" Angelique asked me.

"I'm taking him home," I said. "You take Mom back, Sis. I'll call you later."

12

Nella drove my car, and I got in the backseat with GT's head on my lap. He was shuddering and sweating. He also smelled odd. It was a loamy odor, but I dismissed it. I thought that his hair was still dirty from the graveyard — at least that's what I told myself.

"What's wrong with you, GT?"

"Hungry, Airy. Starving. I've been so happy to see you that I forgot to eat."

"Let's get you something. Nella, stop at the next supermarket."

"No." GT wheezed and stammered.

"What?"

"Take me to the ocean, Airy."

"Why?"

"Take me to the sea."

He shuddered terribly and then went still. He was still breathing. His eyes were open, too. But he didn't say another word, just stared up out of the window. I could see the reflections of the clouds in his clear and glassy eyes.

"Drive out to Santa Monica, Nella," I said.

"What for?"

"Just do it, honey. Just do it."

GT felt hot on my lap. The fever of his attack was taking hold. His eyes slanted at me at one point, and he smiled. The fingers of his left hand stirred, but the hand could not rise.

Nella was a fast driver. She brought us to a parking lot at the shore in under twenty minutes. When I opened the door, GT rose up and dashed out toward the Pacific. As soon as he reached the beach, he dove into the sand headfirst. By the time Nella and I got to him, he had already swallowed a great deal.

I tried to pull his head away, but he threw me off with little more than a shrug. His strength was amazing. By the time I was on him again, he had turned over and was now looking toward the sky. His mouth was caked with sand, but under that you could make out the smile on his face.

"Take me home, Airy," he whispered. "I need to rest."

His eyes closed then. I picked him up in my arms and carried him back to the car. A few bystanders gaped at us, but no one interfered. Nella opened the back door for me, and I laid his unconscious body across the seat.

"Where to?" Nella asked.

"I'll drive" was my answer.

"We should be taking him to the hospital," Nella was saying.

We were on Pico Boulevard, headed for my live-in garage.

"He said that he wanted to go home," I said.

"And what happens if he dies?"

"He's stopped shaking. He's not hot anymore. Maybe he . . ." I tried to think how sand could be a cure for any ailment. "I don't know, Nella. But I'm going to do what he said to do. I don't want the hospital to get him."

"Why not?"

"Because he knows a lot about my family that I don't. And if they get him in there, they might see how crazy he is and keep him from us."

"And you're willing to risk his life for that?"

"I don't think he's going to die," I said. "Damn. Just a few hours ago you were calling him Satan."

"Do you hear those sounds coming out from his gut, Errol?" Nella asked.

I could hear the noise at the red lights with the motor idling. It was a muted thrashing sound, like a dishwasher might make.

"I never seen anybody eat a pint of sand before, either," I said. "It could just be his stomach reacting. That's all."

"All right," she said, throwing up her hands literally and with her tone.

We got him to my place soon after that. It was lucky that I could drive right up to my front door through the driveway. That way no one could see me carrying the comatose GT.

I laid him out on my bed. Nella put her arms around me and kissed my cheek.

"What are you going to do with him, baby?" she asked.

"I don't know. I don't know anything. He knows more about my life than I do. It's crazy."

"Do you want me to stay here with you?"

"No," I told her. "When he gets up I want to talk to him alone."

The exhaustion of the day, the fears and revelations, had sapped my strength. I didn't know what time it was, but the sun was still up. I sat down in the chair next to the bed. Nella kissed my neck. She said something that I didn't understand, and when I looked for her again, she was gone.

GT's stomach was still making that churning sound, though it seemed to be getting softer. He was breathing but otherwise still.

I nodded in the chair, catching myself two or three times. At last, though, I went with it, going all the way to the floor and curling up on the blue shag rug that lay at the foot of the bed.

It was very quiet in my place. Every now and then a truck rumbled down the street, and I'd feel the vibrations in the concrete floor. Light was still filtering in and through the roof window. Birds were chirping outside. As the light faded, I slipped deeper into sleep, and for a long time I felt nothing, thought nothing, and as far as I can remember, I had nary a dream.

A light flickered somewhere. The sudden flash interrupted my sleep but didn't quite bring me to consciousness. I was still under a blanket of slumber but thinking about that light. At first I thought it was a match, someone lighting a cigarette. Then it seemed that the light, once it glimmered, had stayed. Maybe a candle had been lit, I thought. But there were no candles in my place. No fireplace or lantern. Maybe, I thought somewhere near Nod, it was just an electric light. But who could have turned it on? No one. Nella had gone home. But there was someone else. GT. The boy who said he was my father. Who was sick.

Then I felt the hard concrete through the carpet. I opened my eyes and saw the light shining. It still didn't make sense. The luminescence wasn't flame or a lightbulb.

I sat up and saw the bright screen of my computer monitor.

I remembered that I hadn't turned it off, that Shelly had been instant-messaging me. But then GT had run in with his blue towels flowing.

GT was in the same position I'd left him in. If I leaned in close, I could still hear the noises from his stomach, but they were much quieter now.

I went to the toilet to urinate and then came back to the bed, still very tired. I thought for a moment of lying down next to the young stranger who might have been my blood. But I decided that he shouldn't be disturbed.

On my way past the monitor, I saw that Shelly had gone on with her message.

For almost a year I'd hoped for a personal communication from her; just a note of apology or even some angry reason for having left. Instead all I ever got were letters from her lawyer, informing me about the state of our divorce proceedings.

All that time I had been missing her, but right then I barely cared what she had to say. My life had picked up at last and headed on a path that led far away from our union.

13

I know that you don't want to talk to me, Errol. I guess I shouldn't expect anything from you, seeing how I acted. But you have to realize that it caught me off guard as much as it did you. I mean, we were together since the tenth grade. I didn't know anything outside of our relationship. And when I started seeing Tommy he showed me so many things that I never experienced. He knows all of these interesting people and he lives in this great building in New York. And you know I had never had sex with anybody but you. It was so exciting at first. But I see now that it was just different, just sex.

The note broke off there. And then continued again, later, I suppose.

I see that you're still online. I guess this means that you don't want to answer. I was hoping that you'd ask me how I was doing out here. If you had, I would have told you that it's not really working with Tommy and me right now. He's a nice guy and all, but I don't really fit in this world. And he feels guilty about what we did to you. I do too. I'm coming back to Los Angeles for a while. Tommy and I need a little space. I don't know what's going to happen, but I'd like to see you if you want to see me. I'll be at my mother's house a week from Friday. I don't really know how long I'll be there. At least a few weeks, I guess.

"What does it say?" GT asked.

He was standing right behind me. I jumped up from the chair.

"What does it say, Airy? You look so sad."

"Can't you read, GT?" I asked, forgetting all that I had felt just seconds before.

His bright eyes bored into mine. He seemed to be different again. It was as if he were transforming into a new man every few hours.

"Not yet."

"My father could read. He was a very well-read man."

"And I remember every word of it, Airy.

Guy de Maupassant and Zola and Dumas and Márquez. I remember almost word for word Will and Ariel Durant's *Story of Civilization*. But there's a translation connection that hasn't formed yet in my head."

"What are you talking about?" I asked the beautiful youth.

"In some ways, Airy, I'm younger than the baby in your sister's womb. I've just arrived, and all the synapses and little counts haven't yet matched up. That's why I was so lost out there in the graveyard. All I had was your name in my mind. Reading is a complex, nonbiological system. I won't have it back for a while yet. As it is, I'm only now beginning to remember my mission."

"What mission?"

"I don't know, exactly," GT said. "There's something I have to do. Someplace I have to go. Someone I have to become. I don't quite have it, but I will remember. It's only a matter of time."

"Do you want something to drink?" I asked.

The frown of trying to recall his mission reconstructed itself into a smile.

"You bet," he said.

I went to the faucet in the kitchen and poured him a tumbler of water, which he downed as fast as he could swallow. He held the glass out, and we repeated the process.

Halfway through the fifth glass, GT seemed to get his fill. He put the vessel on the drain board and bade me sit next to him at the butcher-block dining table.

"I want you to believe in me, Airy," he said. "I want to prove to you that I am who and what I say I am. Me sitting here in front of you is the most important event in the history of the world. I'm not crazy. I am your father. I was dead and I have risen, even though I never believed in God and I still don't today."

"But, GT." I said the name almost as a talisman to keep his words from infecting my mind. "You haven't said anything to prove you are who you say you are. It's just your face, and as my mother said, you don't have the scar."

"A thousand thousand thousand years ago," he said in a voice that a thespian historian might have used, "there was a great explosion upon the world. Probably a meteorite. And the First Life in all of its simplicity and strength was driven far below into a cavern miles under the surface. There it multiplied and bubbled. There it counted the long moments between where

90

it had been and what it had become. While it was counting, there came an awareness, a knowledge of the selves of numbers. One knew its own count, and so did Two and Three and Four. And when Four knew that it was also One, there was an ecstasy and a motion, and then there was Five."

"What are you saying?" I asked.

"That there is something more than the singular mind. There are connections between moments of awareness that blend together and cannot know blame."

"So you're saying that this First Life thing took over your dead brain and brought you back to life?"

"Yes."

"From all the way down in the middle of the earth?"

"No. For all those years, First Life has been migrating, becoming the Wave. Rising up toward the surface. It washed over what was left of me when I was put in the ground."

"Those are just words, man," I said. "They don't prove anything."

I yawned then. Despite my long nap I was still tired from the past few days. And my two injured fingers were throbbing.

"Listen to me, Airy," GT said. "I'll tell you something that only I could know.

Look under the top center drawer of your mother's bureau in the bedroom. Read what I wrote and see when I wrote it. Look at the pictures, and then dig where I say."

"Top center drawer," I said to make sure I got it right.

"If that doesn't prove it, you will never know happiness."

After that I went to bed. GT said he'd rested enough and that he wanted to stare at my books to see if he could remember how to read.

From the moment my head hit the pillow, I was asleep. I dreamed about Shelly. She was on her knees before Thomas Willens. He had a huge black erection (which was odd, because he's a white guy), and she was naked with her hands tied behind her back. She was sucking and kissing his hard-on passionately. It was as if she had been starving and this was her first meal in many days.

14

GT was gone when I woke up. He had taken *One Hundred Years of Solitude* from its place on the shelf. There was also a sweater missing, but he'd left my tennis shoes.

Shelly hadn't sent me any more notes, so I logged off. I made a bowl of sweet oatmeal and topped that with sliced bananas that I grilled in the broiler. But by the time I sat down to eat, I had no appetite.

When I was in the shower, the bandage on my sliced finger lost its stick and fell off. That was the first time I realized that my hands no longer hurt. You could still see where the razor wire had cut, but the skin underneath had healed. The swelling was gone. There was crust from the scab, but that just brushed off like sand. My smashed nail was almost completely healed. I remember thinking that at least I was healing well.

I seemed to be over Shelly, and Nella was now in my life. The crazy kid was gone. Maybe I'd even call AT&T and get a job working in Visual Basic or Web design.

It wasn't until about ten that I thought about the top center drawer of my mother's bureau.

I loved my mother, but she had always been distant, like the moon. I had never had long talks with her, and she didn't seem to understand emotional pain. If I was sick, she'd take my temperature. If I had a fever, she gave me children's aspirin. But if I was heartbroken over some little girl, she'd just say, "In a hundred years, none of this will matter."

I had always thought that my mother was immune to passionate love. That's why the thought of her having an affair was so strange to me. Her role was one of regularity and emotional invulnerability.

She went to work at the *Olympic Gazette* every morning at eight-thirty, came home for a forty-five-minute lunch at one, and then went back to work until at least six but more often until eight or nine. She never got sick or lazy. She never varied her schedule for anything unless somebody in the family was ill.

I hurried off to the pottery studio and had finished most of my chores before Nella arrived.

Instead of saying hello, she kissed me. I liked that.

"He's gone," I said.

"Your father?"

"GT. He took a book and a sweater and went on his way."

"No. He wouldn't do something like that." Nella's disbelief almost convinced me that he might be there when I returned home.

"You sound like you know him," I said.

"He talked a lot while you were getting your mother," Nella said. "He told us about the giant life of numbers under the ground. He said that that life was bubbling up and all of our fears for all the years we've been here would soon melt away. He said that all of the dreams human beings have had would be realized and then seen as paltry things."

"And that means he wouldn't just leave?"

"He told us how much he loved you and Angelique. He wanted to spend time with you."

"But did he tell you about his mission?" I asked.

"No."

"Last night he said that he'd been given a mission. But that he didn't remember what it was yet."

"What mission?"

"Yeah. One shudders to think."

"Is that why you're here so early?" Nella asked me. "Because your father was gone and you were lonely?"

"He's not my father. He's a nut. And I came in early because I have to go do something."

"What?"

"File my divorce papers."

"Oh." Nella smiled. "Now that you're a free man, you will want to bed every woman you can."

"Yeah," I said. "I'm going to sleep with a hundred women. All of them named Nella Bombury."

That made the island woman grin.

I got to my mother's apartment at 1:55. My sister and I both had keys. I knocked to be sure, but nobody answered. I went in through the front door and down the left hall, which ended at my parents' door. The furniture in my parents' bedroom had not changed since I could remember. There was a queen-size bed, a small maple desk, and a maple bureau with a wide mirror and three rows of drawers. I pulled out the top middle drawer, half expecting to find nothing while hoping for another memory from my father through his bastard son.

There was a manila folder taped to the underside of the drawer. The tape was yellowed and brittle. It had obviously been there for many years. The tape broke away when I tried to peel it off, and the folder fell into my hands. I sat there in a half-lotus position, afraid, suddenly, of what I might have found.

There was a full-length mirror leaned up against the wall across from me. I watched myself for a moment or two, wondering how I might have kept from coming to this place and time. Maybe if I hadn't gone to the graveyard. I tried to think my way back to that decision, but it was gone, and I was there like a thief in my mother's house, unable to stop moving forward.

The folder contained a dozen eight-and-a-half-by-eleven glossy black-and-white photographs and a letter penned in purple ink.

The detective had found a way to put a hole in the wall of the motel room where my mother and Bobby Bliss had their trysts. He had probably taken hundreds of photos, but these twelve were certainly the most damning.

At first I didn't think it was my mother. Maybe, I thought, the detective had fooled my father by showing him pictures of another woman with Bobby Bliss — a woman who resembled his wife. But looking closer, I saw that it was her. It was just that she was unfamiliar to me because I'd never seen that kind of ardor in her face. One shot after another showed her contorted visage, her adoring his erection, her slung over his shoulder, her screaming and begging for his touch.

My mother's lover was a bronze-colored man with a shaven head and big muscles. He had a thick mustache that would have made women think he was handsome.

I imagined how my father must have felt and how my mother would feel if she knew that pictures like this existed. I determined never to tell her.

But that was before I read the letter.

September 19, 1984

This letter is a confession penned by Arthur Bontemps Porter III on the date above. I write these words while my wife is sleeping in her bed. Our bed. I don't know who will read this or under what circumstances, but these are the pictures that have driven me to a terrible act. My wife has made me a cuckold and has therefore given me no other way out.

The man in the pictures with Maddie is Robert Randolph Bliss, an unemployed maintenance man who lived in Culver City. For a short while he worked at the hospital where my wife's brother was operated on. I suppose that is where the affair began. I think it must have gone on for a long time. For months I suspected but said nothing. When I finally confronted her, she lied and said that they had parted. But while I was at work, they would still meet. I hired the detective and he brought me the proof.

I went to Mr. Bliss and offered him twenty-five thousand dollars to break it off with my wife. I told him that I wanted a letter from him that I could deliver into her hands. The letter would say that he was leaving her, that he never loved her.

I had saved that twenty-five thousand for us to travel around the world, first-class. But I was willing to throw it away on revenge.

I met Bliss in our home while my wife was away, thinking she was going to meet him. He made a date with her and then brought me the letter. I gave him the cash in a big plastic folder. While he was counting his lucre, I shot him in the left eye.

I buried him, along with all the other evidence, under the wood floor of the back room in the garage.

I put Bliss's note in an envelope with Maddie's name typed on it, and sealed it. When she came home, I gave it to her. I told her that I found the note under our door when I came home. She cried all night, telling me that it was her time of month. I comforted her with a whiskey and some nice words, knowing all the while that I had slaughtered her Mr. Bliss and put him in a garbage-bag coffin not ten feet from where she started her car.

In the next few months she will be sad. Bliss's family, if he has any, will also rue his disappearance.

He's dead and gone and Maddie is inconsolable.

I've had my revenge but I feel no better for the retribution. I realize that she was lost to me before ever meeting that man. Now that I have *killed him, I know that if he were alive again, I'd let him live. Because I know now that there is no cure for the pain.*

Arthur Bontemps Porter III

The floorboards were loose in the toolroom at the back of the garage. I cleared the dirt away from the corpse with only a broom. He was wrapped in six garbage bags tied together in the center to keep him from smelling up the area. The skin had shrunk up next to his bones. Upon his chest lay a corroded .22 pistol, the murder weapon. Next to the body bags was a plastic envelope that held the twenty-five thousand dollars, all in twenty-dollar bills.

The guilt my father felt kept him from holding on to the money. He probably threw it down in a last moment of passion. Or maybe he buried it later, hoping somehow to serve penance for the damage he'd done.

15

"It is a crime to disturb a crime scene, Mr. Porter," Detective Lehman Burke said to me a few days later.

I was sitting in the third-floor interrogation room of the Wilshire Precinct.

I had called the police the day after finding the letter and the corpse. At first I thought that I could just let it go. It was a crime of passion, committed over twenty years ago. The murderer was dead, had been for nine years.

I couldn't sleep at all that night. I kept remembering my father's brief reference to Bobby Bliss's family. His mother or sister or maybe even his children who never knew what became of him.

The next morning I went to my mother after a brief visit with Nella.

My mom read the letter once and handed it back to me.

"That boy told you about this?" she asked.

"Uh-huh."

"Where is he now?"

"I don't know."

"Call the police," she told me.

And I did.

"I know that, Officer Burke," I said. "But you have to understand. The person who told me about the letter was very irresponsible, and I had no reason to believe that Mr. Bliss was actually dead. As a matter of fact, I had never heard of him before a few days ago."

"You should have called the police," he insisted.

"Well, I didn't," I said. "I looked where the letter said to look."

"And you didn't call us for twenty-four hours," Burke added.

"I know. I didn't see where it mattered. That man was my mother's lover, and he was murdered by my father. You can see where I might have had some conflict at bringing up so much pain."

"The law is the law, Mr. Porter."

Burke was a Negro, as am I. The same tone but not the same color, exactly. Where my skin has a maple-brown hue, he had more of an ashen undertone. He had a slender build and a thick mustache like Bobby Bliss had. He smoked one cigarette after another directly under a NO SMOKING sign, but I didn't complain.

"Did you find anything in the grave with him?" Burke asked. "Other than the gun, I mean."

"No. Like what?"

"I don't know. He said in the note that he put all the evidence in the grave with Bliss. Sounds to me like he could have meant the money."

"I don't know what he did with the money," I said. "I have no idea."

Burke stared hard at me.

I tried not to look guilty.

Finally he said, "Tell me more about this young man you call GT."

I went through the story again, telling him about the late-night calls and the meeting at the graveyard. I told him about all the things GT seemed to know concerning our family and my suspicion that he was the son of a second family in Georgia.

"And he was the one who told you about this letter?" Burke asked for the twentieth time.

"Yes. He told me about it the night before he left."

"On his mission?"

"Yes."

"It sounds crazy," Burke said. Then he paused to see if I wanted to change any part of my story.

"It sure does," I agreed.

"And you didn't find any money in the grave?"

"No, sir."

"And you knew nothing about the murder before you read the letter?"

"I was a child when that letter was written."

"And you have no idea who this GT is?"

"He told me that he was my father," I said. "He said that he rose up out of the grave."

"And you say he stayed at your apartment for a few days?"

"Two," I said. "Two days."

"Mr. Porter," Burke said rather formally, "would you give a team of my men permission to search your house?"

"My house? The body was at my mother's place. He's been dead twenty years. What could you possibly find at my house?"

"So you refuse?" Detective Burke inquired.

"No," I said. "I can even tell you there's a tumbler on my sink that GT was the last one to touch. I haven't been to my house much since the body was found. My mom, you know. She needs the company."

And that was that. The police took my

keys and searched the house, looking for GT's fingerprints and maybe the cash my father mentioned. My mother, who had always been removed and aloof, entered a period of grief that made her seem like a completely different woman. She'd read my father's confession many times over. She even went out to see the body before the police came.

"What did you think happened to him?" I asked her on the first night after she learned about the murder.

"I thought he'd left me. That's what the note said."

"And you never suspected anything?"

"No," she said.

"Did you love him?"

She was silent for many long minutes before answering. "Bobby was a wild man. He carried a straight razor in his pocket and sometimes a gun. He was working as a janitor at the hospital where Uncle Mortie had gone for open-heart surgery. He was nice to me, and after Mortie got better, Bobby called one day. He said that he was in the neighborhood and wanted to drop by. For some reason, I just couldn't say no."

"He was so wild that you thought he might just have run away one day?" I asked.

"I don't know. I was so sad, and your father was very kind to me." My mother had a broken look. "Now I suppose that was all guilt. But I'm sure those pictures cut him way down deep."

"Why didn't you and Dad break up?"

"We loved each other in our own way," she said. "And . . . and . . . there was you and Angie. Our problems didn't have to be yours, too."

I took the twenty-five thousand dollars to Nella's house right after I decided to tell my mother about the crime. I told Nella that she could have three thousand just to hold on to it for me.

"I'll hold *all* of it," Nella told me. "I only take what money I have earned."

I don't know why I took the money. Maybe I was afraid the police would have kept it, or maybe I thought that seeing the money Bobby Bliss agreed to take would break my mother's heart. But looking back on it, I guess it was because I was so broke, and in some way it felt like a gift from my father to keep me from sinking too low.

Except for the past mayhem, things weren't too bad. GT was gone. The world was looking better. I had a line of gold-

and-green celadon-glazed mugs thrown on the wheel and then altered to look something like fat Chinese ducks. I'd thrown and fired over six hundred mugs and planned to sell them at the street fair for twelve dollars each. It wasn't a lot of money, after expenses, but at least it was a start.

I visited Angie a little more often, and about every other night I spent wining and dining the lovely Ms. Bombury with money I'd stolen from a murdered man's grave.

16

The phone rang at two-thirty the morning before the crafts sale. I was up wrapping and boxing mugs for the show. The bell at that hour gave me a chill. As the days had gone by, I'd begun to be afraid of GT. He was obviously crazy; mentally unstable and physically very strong — a bad combination. He had information about me and my family that I'd never suspected. And even though I knew he couldn't have had anything to do with Bobby Bliss's death, I still associated him with that violent act.

I let the phone go to the answering machine so as not to have to speak if it was GT on the line.

"Errol, this is Lon. If you're there, pick up."

There was noise in the background that made it plain my sister's husband wasn't calling from their home.

"What is it, Lon?"

"It's Anj. She's real sick."

"Where are you?"

"At the hospital. Temple. They admitted her through the emergency room."

"I'll be right there."

By the time I got to the admissions desk of the emergency room, it was almost three-thirty. Lon was nodding in a chair between a nauseated-looking woman and a man with a bloody gauze bandage wrapped around his forearm.

"She got these terrible pains and started bleeding," Lon said. "I brought her here, and they took her right in. The doctors haven't said a thing."

"What are they doing for her?" I asked.

"I think they're operating. That's what the nurse said."

"When did she start bleeding?"

"It started about nine. I brought her in because we thought it might be some kind of rough labor or something, but they said that the bleeding was bad."

Lon was tall and prematurely gray. He had a young face, though, and an athletic physique. We never liked each other much. It didn't have anything to do with race or even with my sister. We were just very different people. But he was my brother-in-law, so I treated him as well as I could.

"Who's in charge of the operation?" I asked.

"I don't know anything else, Errol," Lon said. "They just put me off whenever I go up to the desk."

I went up. They put me off, too.

"I'm sorry, Mr. Porter," a young Latina in a white uniform told me. "Your sister is very sick, and Dr. Valeria is operating on her now. We won't know anything until she comes out of surgery. We might not know anything certain for a few days."

"What about the baby?" I asked.

"I don't know," she said. "You'll have to excuse me."

Lon and I waited until six-thirty. After the doctor had a brief conference with us, I called Nella.

I told her what happened and then asked, "Could you go by my house and pick up a few of my boxes? I'm stuck at the hospital, waiting to see what's happening. The key is in the iron lamp up over the left side of the door."

"Is she going to be all right?" Nella asked.

"They say she has a pretty good chance, but they're not sure about the baby. They removed her from Angie's womb. She's only two and a quarter pounds. They put her in an incubator."

"I'll pick up your boxes, Errol. But after this, I t'ink you better t'ink about goin' to church."

"I promise," I said.

I really meant it, too. My life up to the age of twenty-seven had gone off without a hitch, except for the death of my father. I'd gotten good grades at school and college. I'd married my high school sweetheart, fallen into a great job . . . Then all of a sudden things started going wrong.

Maybe it was time to get into a fold.

At 8:05, Dr. Valeria came out to meet with us for the second time.

"She's very sick," the olive-skinned European said. "But she's stable now. The bleeding has stopped, and the baby is breathing on life support. All we can do now is to give their bodies the chance to work their magic."

"Isn't there some medicine?" Lon asked. "Something you can do?"

The doctor shook his head. His wiry copper-colored hair shimmered as he moved.

"No," he said. "They are both very weak. We will keep them warm, keep them quiet

112

and clean. Wait twenty-four hours and then we will see how to proceed."

Valeria told us that we wouldn't be able to see Angie or the baby for at least forty-eight hours, so Lon went back to the waiting room, and I left for the street fair.

I had shared the cost of the booth with Nella. It was a big one, costing four hundred and fifty dollars for the two days. Nella had all the materials. It looked pretty cool. Like a big tent with shelves and free-standing displays.

Nella's work was large. Handmade mythical animals designed with complex pastel patterns. She also made oversize stoneware platters that had been thrown and then reworked into large ovals and other, more complex shapes like whales and undulating rivers.

Nella's work took up most of the space, so she paid for most of it. My mugs were on a few shelves along the side.

"How is your sister?" she asked me when I arrived.

"Alive," I said. "The doctors don't know what will happen. They have her in the ICU for the next forty-eight hours, at least."

"And her baby?"

"On life support, too."

Nella put her arms around me. I think she expected me to cry, but I couldn't. I was just taking steps one after another. I couldn't imagine anything happening to Angie. That just wasn't a possibility.

"She's going to be fine," I said. "Don't you worry."

The words were dead on my tongue, but I don't think Nella realized that.

"Let's get to work," she said, putting away the pain she felt for me. "I already sold four of your ugly mugs."

"Really? Damn."

The day went along quite well. By two I'd sold over 130 mugs, and Nella had moved five platters. We'd made about the same amount of money, because Nella's plates cost three hundred dollars each.

Every hour I called the hospital, but Angelique's condition had remained the same.

Nella had just gone out to walk around the fair "to scope out the competition," when the three men in suits came into the tent. I realized later that they must have been watching, waiting for Nella or me to walk away.

Two of them seemed to be cast from the

same mold. Dark suits. Tall and white with every hair and crease in place. The last man was tall also, but his light-colored suit was ill-fitting — loose in the chest and tight at the waist.

The twins wandered around a bit and then settled near the entrance. There they pulled the canvas flap across the front, closing off the space to the public. I was about to ask them to move the fabric door back, when the man in the bad suit came up to me. He had one of my mugs in his hand.

"Mr. Porter?" he said.

"Yes?"

"My name is Werner."

He had robin's-egg-blue eyes and a craggy face that if it had been on a marble facade, you might have said got only the first treatment of sandblasting. The skin was pocked and mottled.

"We have a problem," Werner said.

"What's that?"

"We're looking for your father. Do you know where he is?"

"In the grave," I said. The cold in my gut almost doubled me over.

The ugly stone face smiled.

"This is no time for artifice, young man."

"I don't know what the fuck you're talking about, mister. My father died nine years ago."

"Then why, may I ask, were his fingerprints found on a water glass in your house just recently?"

17

They identified themselves as government agents but demurred when I asked what agency they worked for. They used a plastic tie to secure my wrists behind my back, then hurried me out of the street fair and into a black Lincoln Town Car. The dark-suited twins got in the front seat, while the lumpy agent sat next to me in back.

"Can I see your identification again, Agent Werner?" I asked him.

"You don't need to see my identification," he said. "You need to get your story straight."

"But —"

"Wait until we get there," he said.

It was a very long drive. Because the men refused to answer my questions, I leaned my temple against the cold door-glass and closed my eyes. I imagined a vast blue sky with two great clouds. One was in the shape of a white rhinoceros, and the other was a feral snow hare. The winds blew the clouds together at an excruciatingly sluggish rate. Slowly, as they came together, the animals became a great blue-on-blue dragon.

I couldn't shake the vision. It wasn't a dream or a mental construction. I thought at the time that it was a symptom of the great stress I was under, a way to escape my helplessness.

At last we arrived at a house near the outskirts of Ventura, in a rural town called Fillmore. It had once been a working orange farm. There were still hundreds of citrus trees surrounding the house. The property was immense for a single dwelling, almost the size of a plantation. There were certainly no next-door neighbors to peek over the fence and ask what was going on.

I was dragged into the adobe-style mansion and deposited on a large, shaggy sofa. It was white and smelled of cured wool.

Werner sat on a hassock in front of me. I was leaning on my side because it was hard to sit upright with my hands restricted.

"This is no joke," he said.

"What's your first name?" I asked him.

"Jim."

"Well, Agent Jim, I have no jokes to tell."

"Then let's drop this shit about your father being dead, shall we?" he suggested.

"There was a man at my house," I said as calmly as I could. "He claimed to be my father. But he was no more than twenty."

"Where'd you meet this guy?" James Werner asked me.

"He called me," I said. "Crazy, hopeless kinds of calls. I went out and found him in the graveyard."

"What was he doing there?"

"I don't know. Sleeping on my father's grave."

"You say that he looked like he was a young man?"

"Absolutely. Almost a boy. But strong."

"How do you know that?"

I related the experience of GT throwing me at the beach.

"Why was he eating sand?" Agent Jim asked.

"He was crazy," I said. "Like I told you."

The rock-faced government agent stared hard at me. He seemed to come to some kind of conclusion and nodded. He stood up, snipped the tie holding my wrists, and left the room, closing the door behind him.

The room he left me in had five doors, all of which were closed, and a big window looking out on a pair of weeping willows. The doors were locked. The windows were all barred by ornate cast-iron gratings that were painted pink. I wandered over to the shelf above the fireplace. There was a line of about twenty books between bookends made from bronze replicas of Remington cowboys atop bucking steeds.

Most of the books were male-oriented adventures. Books about submarines at war, World War II battles, and Civil War strategies. There was one book that was different. It was a slender tome on astrophysics entitled *The Effect of Celestial Events on the Biosphere.* The subject was the impact of meteorites that have struck the earth and altered the environment and life.

I remembered GT's claim about an explosion, probably a meteorite, and felt a sudden chill. Despite all the evidence that had been presented to me up until that moment, it was seeing that book that made me wonder if what GT had been saying might really be true.

I didn't understand most of what I read of the introduction, but I got enough to glean a postulation about a meteorite that had struck Earth one and a half billion years ago. This rock was four times the size of the one they thought wiped out the dinosaurs. There were no large animals at that time, only single-celled, bacteria-like creatures. Dr. Zellman, the author, speculated that such life would both survive and be deeply altered by such a dramatic change in environment —

"Good evening, Mr. Porter," a man's voice said.

When I looked up, I realized that the sun had gone down. I had been on the sheepskin couch reading for some time.

The man standing before me was tall and slender with a rather elevated forehead. He was over forty but not yet fifty. His eyes were dark, maybe green, and intense.

"Who are you?"

"David Wheeler," he said with no hint of humor. "I will be your host for the next few days."

"I can't stay here," I said. "My sister's sick, and I'm running a pottery sale with a friend."

"The sale has been going quite well," Wheeler said. "And your sister is still in the ICU with her child. As soon as we know anything about their condition, you will be informed."

"You can't just hold me here," I said.

"The man you say claimed to be your father stayed with you for a couple of days?" Wheeler asked.

"Yeah."

"Was he ever wounded during that time period?"

"What do you mean?"

"Was he cut, bruised, lacerated?"

"Why would something like that happen to him?"

"I'm not blaming you for anything, Mr. Porter," my interlocutor assured me. "I was just wondering if he healed quickly."

I thought about my finger. *I* had healed at an incredible rate.

"No," I said. "No, uh-uh. I mean, I can't say if he healed quickly, because nothing ever happened to him. Why do you ask?"

"Did your father —"

"GT," I said. "I called him GT."

"Why did you call him that?"

"When I met him, he kept saying that good times were coming."

Wheeler frowned.

"Did this GT tell you where he came from?"

"He said that he was my father," I said. "That he'd risen from the grave. He called me from the graveyard."

"How did he have your number?"

"I'm listed. He probably called information. But let me ask you something, Mr. Wheeler —"

"Dr. Wheeler," he corrected.

"Let me ask you something, Doctor."

"What is that?"

"Agent Werner said that the fingerprints on the glass on my sink belonged to my father. Is that true?"

"Did this GT resemble your father?" he asked instead of answering me.

"A little bit. I figured that he was the illegitimate son of my old man."

"Do you honestly believe that your father would have maintained a separate family outside of your own?"

"Ask me if I believe that my father would have murdered my mother's lover and then buried him in the garage."

Wheeler had been standing all this time. He wore soft, dark maroon trousers and a square-cut yellow shirt meant to hang out of the pants. His shoes were alligator, and there was a thick and cloudy crystal ring on his left pinky.

"May I sit, Mr. Porter?"

"It's your house, man."

He sat on a stuffed chair across from me.

"You don't believe that men can rise up out of the grave?" he asked.

"No."

"But didn't this GT tell you things that only your father could have known?"

"Yes," I said. "But my father could have told GT or GT's mother those stories."

"You think that he would have admitted

committing a murder to a woman who may very well have wanted him for her own?"

He was fondling the opaque crystal ring with the fingers of his right hand.

"People do all kinds of crazy things," I said.

Wheeler shook his extra-long head. "You're too bright to believe that," he said. "Top of your class in computer science at UCLA. An excellent chess player."

"Then why don't you believe me?" I asked.

Wheeler sat up straight and put his hands on his knees. He fixed me with his maybe-green eyes and said, "Those were your father's fingerprints on that glass. We've exhumed his grave, and all that's left in the coffin is fine white sand."

Images of my father, the old man, flooded my mind. Along with these images were flashes of GT with all of his boyish exuberance. There were those phone calls from the graveyard and the insults I had piled upon him.

Wheeler was handing me a handkerchief.

I hadn't even known that tears were streaming down my face.

"Come with me, Errol," Dr. Wheeler said. "I want to show you some things that will surprise you."

18

We exited through the back of the residence. There was a good-looking forty-something woman working in a large garden. Her tan was heavily laden with freckles, and her biceps and calves were dense from physical labor. She looked at us and waved. Neither Dr. Wheeler nor I responded, but she smiled anyway.

There were two men in army fatigues waiting next to a bright lemon-yellow convertible Hummer parked outside the gate to the garden.

"We're going to take a little drive," Wheeler informed me.

He and I climbed into the backseat while the brawny white soldiers got in front.

We traveled over wide plains and dirt paths carved into forest landscapes. For a mile or two, we drove along the beach. We may not have gone any more than ten or twelve miles from the defunct orange grove, but it took us over an hour.

I didn't mind. It was a clear day, and the breeze was exhilarating. The sun's rays shone like crystals in the air. I could see sections of the sky that were different from each other. Some were orange, others violet.

The mild hallucination didn't bother me at the time.

"Here we are," Wheeler said.

We had pulled up in front of a large concrete bunker. Gray and rough around the edges, it was somewhat reminiscent of the face of the agent who had arrested me — James Werner.

"What is it?" I asked.

The soldiers had jumped out. One of them helped me down. I got the feeling that his supportive hand would have turned into a vise in an instant if I resisted.

There was a steel door to the bunker. It was painted drab green with PROPERTY OF THE U.S. GOVERNMENT printed across it in red.

The door opened as we approached, but there were no obvious sentries.

We walked down a close concrete hallway and then entered an elevator that was built like a cage. The car descended a hundred or more feet, depositing us in a dark chamber that had only one blue light for illumination. The luminescence allowed me to see the men I had come with, but it was too weak to light up the room.

"Is this the man, sir?" a voice boomed from somewhere.

"Yes, it is."

"Then shall we execute the process?"

"I believe we shall," Wheeler said ominously.

I didn't like the word *execute,* especially when the soldiers grabbed me by both arms. A bank of bright lights came on with a bang and a flash. The soldiers dragged me along without saying a word, heedless of my frightened complaints.

I let my weight go dead, but that had little effect on the men *executing* their *process.*

While they dragged me along I thought about my sister. I wondered if she were doing well after the surgery, if she had survived. I decided that if she died while Wheeler had me locked away in his paranoid dugout, I would come after him. I would come up on him one day in surprise and shoot him through his left eye.

The hatred that rose up in me, the anger that burned in my heart — it wasn't mine. I knew that as clearly as I knew the difference between my foot and the sock covering it. But for a moment rage and lust for retribution were all I knew.

★ ★ ★

We came to an infirmary with a long table and a few empty cots. The light here was low, but I could make out a man in a white doctor's smock that was open, revealing his suit pants. He was a middle-aged man with small eyes and huge hands.

"What's the goddamn emergency, Wheeler?" the doctor said. "I've been co-ordinating the presentation without you."

"Dr. Gregory, I'd like you to meet Errol Porter, the son of XT-248."

"I thought we weren't notifying the families, David?" the doctor replied.

"XT-248 called Errol."

The room was dark, but Gregory was definitely a white man; even in that dim light, I could see the blood drain from his face. He put his hand on the examination table to steady himself.

"What?"

"We need the full blood workup within the hour."

The moment he uttered these words, the soldiers tightened their grip.

"And then," Wheeler added, "we'll take him to the pit — one way or the other."

I was thrown on a gurney and secured by small straps at my feet and ankles, and also by larger restraints across my chest and

128

thighs. Dr. Gregory started almost immediately cutting off my clothes with a small pair of scissors. He was good at this but also rather callous. He cut my skin a few times, the way a sheepshearer might nick an ewe. After he'd cut me, he slapped on a dab of plasterlike material that stung — to stanch the bleeding.

I cried out in complaint and demanded my rights, but the doctor and his military aides didn't pay one bit of attention. They treated me as if I actually were a bleating sheep.

They rubbed my body with circular pieces of cloth that they shoved into the drawer of a big machine. Every time they did this, an amber light would come on. They took swabs of my chest and neck, hair and soles, rectum and genitals. Toward the end of this humiliating examination, the doctor began taking blood. He took ten samples, connecting each one to a different tube that came out of the big machine with the amber light.

Then he began examining my body with a Sherlock Holmes–like magnifying glass. It felt as if he were scanning each and every pore and follicle. When he got to my wounded finger, he asked, "When did you get this injury?"

"About seven weeks ago," I lied. "It was at the pottery studio. One of the wires I use to cut the pot from the wheel had frayed, and the wheel started moving fast —"

"What about this nail injury?" he asked, interrupting my overly elaborate fabrication.

"That was about a week ago. I was arguing with XT-248 on the phone and —"

"What do you know about XT-248?" he snapped.

"That's what you called him. He said that he was my father. You seem to think that he was, too. But all I knew was that he was a twenty-year-old kid who's crazy on the streets of L.A."

"All clear," a mechanical female voice declared.

Dr. Gregory, who was staring hard at me, said, "Release him and get him some gear. I'll guess that Wheeler wants him in the pit as soon as possible."

19

I was given a suit of blue pajamas that came with a like-colored pair of paper slippers and an orange sash. The soldiers accompanied me down a long hall and into a wide, brightly lit chamber.

The room was circular with a hole over twenty feet wide in the center. The hole was surrounded by eight-foot razor-wire fencing. The room was over sixty feet in diameter. And it was not empty. A group of people was milling around, more than fifty of them. Everyone except for the soldiers and Drs. Gregory and Wheeler was attired in pajamas of various hues. I hadn't seen Gregory come in, but he was there talking to Wheeler. They were standing next to a large machine that I assumed was a computer.

David Wheeler smiled and approached me.

"Dr. G. gives you a clean bill of health, Errol," he said.

"What does that get me?"

"Come over here and I'll show you."

131

My captor led me to the edge of the vicious fence. The hollow was about thirty feet deep, and the floor was somewhat wider than the top. I could see several subterranean cavities leading from the room.

In the center of the chamber was a small child with her arms and legs manacled and connected to a circular metal brace. Her limbs were stretched to their limit, and she was naked.

"That might have been you," Wheeler whispered in my ear.

"What the fuck is this?" I replied.

"Survival, my friend," Wheeler said in an assured voice. "Survival."

"Shall we go on with the next test, Doctor?" a bodiless, amplified voice requested.

"Yes," Gregory and Wheeler said together.

Pajama-wearing people, both men and women, crowded around the pit. They gazed down in anticipation.

A brawny soldier came out, dressed only in fatigue trousers and armed with a glistening bayonet.

"No!" the child screamed. "Please don't hurt me. Please don't."

The soldier approached cautiously, even hesitantly. I thought at the time that his humanitarian side was holding him back.

The child, who seemed as helpless as she was naked, looked up among the faces of her persecutors. When her gaze came to me, she stared into my eyes. I felt a vibration at the back of my neck. The next thing I knew, I felt compelled to climb the fence, to jump down into that pit and free the child. I fought the urge. I kept fighting it, but the command seemed to be taking me over.

The loudspeaker said, "Now, Jennings," and the girl's attention turned back to her torturer.

He moved quickly, lopping off her right arm with a single thrust.

"No!" I cried. I was not the only viewer so affected.

"Stop this!" someone said.

"This is inhuman!" a woman shouted.

Three or four voices cried out in languages that I didn't understand.

"Please," David Wheeler said, holding his hands above his head. "Watch and learn what it is we are facing."

The little girl was screaming loudly, using her remaining limbs to struggle against her bonds. She was bleeding, but not as much as I would have expected. She cried first in fear and pain and then in anger.

"You fools!" she spat. "You parasites. You troglodytes. You miserable scum. You have a path of diamonds at your feet, and you shit on it and plaster it over with your stench and fear and stupidity."

"Look," one of the women said, pointing to a monitor at the top of the depression.

It was a close-up of the little girl's wound. From the center, where the bone had been visible, a small hand had formed. An arm was growing back from the bloody stump.

The girl kept struggling. The hubbub among the throng grew. The girl looked at me again, but this time there was no compulsion, just sorrow emanating from those eyes.

Suddenly the soldier screamed and rushed at the little girl. He began hacking at her with his razor-sharp bayonet. Off came her legs and remaining arm, off came her screaming head. He hacked away at the pieces on the ground until two more soldiers ran in and held him back.

Grim silence fell upon the crowd of on-lookers. A woman near me went to her knees vomiting. My tongue had gone dry and the back of my neck quivered uncontrollably.

"Mon Dieu," a man behind me uttered.

On the floor below an ever-widening circle of blood spread out from the flesh of the dismembered child. Her mouth opened spasmodically as if she were trying to speak. Her eyes, open wide, once again were gazing at me.

"Cut the pit lights," David Wheeler commanded.

There was a loud clacking sound and the scene of bloody murder went black.

"Everyone listen to me," Wheeler was saying. "What you have seen is terrible. The soldier that committed this atrocity lost control of himself. But do not let your eyes deceive you. It was not a child that was slaughtered before you, but a monster in the guise of innocence . . ."

Is he insane? I thought.

"You saw the arm regenerating," Wheeler continued. "That was the least of this creature's powers. Follow me and I will show you that your fear at this moment is nothing compared to the threat you face."

The crowd was ushered through a door into a large amphitheater. Many complained loudly, shouting for law enforcement and to be allowed to leave. But armed soldiers blocked the exits, and sooner or later, everyone sat down and faced the small circular stage. David Wheeler stood quietly on the dais, before a blond-wood podium, waiting for the outraged audience to quiet down. He never once asked for silence, just stood there looking from side to side.

Finally, when only a few shattered souls were babbling, he said, "You have just witnessed the greatest threat that the human race has ever faced."

I remember thinking that it was the mad soldier he was referring to. But the picture of the little girl in a plaid dress appeared on a large screen behind him.

"MaryBeth Coulder was born on June sixteenth, 1990. She died five years later and was interred in the Evermore Cemetery. She climbed out of that grave fourteen months ago."

While the crowd muttered and complained, pictures of the child's corpse, her interred in a coffin, and finally, the coffin being lowered into the grave were flashed on the screen in succession.

A complete hush settled in amid the throng.

"Why did you have to kill her?" a solitary voice asked.

"As I told you before, Major Jennings lost his mind in there, seeing the monster that MaryBeth had become. He will be relieved. But to answer another question, she did not die under that assault. The spores that animated her corpse are still active in a vault far below this room. We aren't yet sure, but we believe that the body of this girl will rise again from the blood and muck she left behind."

"Impossible."

"Nothing on God's green earth," Dr. Wheeler said, "is impossible. You saw the hand growing back. You saw how a wound that would kill a normal human only served to enrage that creature. And you don't have to take my word for it. Under this facility, we have more than two hundred ghouls in custody. All of them part of an invasion force, the likes of which the world has never known."

"That's crazy, man," a man with a Scottish accent proclaimed.

Others voiced their doubt, but Wheeler smiled upon them. He raised his hands to the level of his chest to ask for silence and got it.

"You are all important members of the international community," he said. "Capitalists and ambassadors, royalty and revolutionaries — you have all been invited by our government to see for yourselves the threat that faces our world. It is true that there have been moments when the United States government has taken the initiative, and when the rest of the world has questioned our authority. This time, however, we don't want to make any mistakes. No public bickering, no petty blame by potentates and socialists. The threat that faces our world is clear and present. Without immediate action, civilization as we know it — mankind itself — may soon be destroyed.

"So that you might see the threat firsthand, Dr. Gregory and I will lead you through the underground prison where we have detained these agents. Please, all of you follow Dr. Gregory. He's standing over there at the west door."

I trailed the group. Somewhere along the way, completely beyond my control, I had fallen into an insanity from which there seemed to be no escape.

Wheeler came up beside me.

"What do you think about your GT now?" he asked.

"I didn't see him torturing small animals."

"They don't feel pain," Wheeler said with an affable smile.

He stopped walking and put a hand on my arm.

"You have stumbled upon the most important event in the history of mankind," he said. "The pyramids, Pompeii, even Jesus Christ himself didn't hold a candle to what happens today in these corridors. Every man and woman in this bunker will be remembered over ten thousand years for what we decide."

There was definitely a deep passion in Wheeler's voice. I wasn't sure if it was tinged with madness.

"Why would the government bring the rest of the world in to see something so . . . so dangerous?" I asked. I didn't really care about his answer; I was just afraid that if I didn't seem somehow interested, he'd have me manacled and amputated.

"We need the scientific community of the entire world behind us, working with us," he said. "And we need eyes around the world to make sure that the contagion is not rising in some other part of the globe."

Contagion?

"And why am I here?" I asked with hardly a tremor.

"You, my friend, are even more rare than the spores that spawn these demons."

"How's that?"

"You are their only human friend," he said with a wolfish smile. "Come on, let's join the others."

20

Wheeler and Gregory led us down a wide tunnel that spiraled like a corkscrew into the earth. Every twenty feet or so was an armed sentry standing against one side of the passageway or the other. These uniformed soldiers all carried automatic weapons and wore body armor.

At last we came to a gigantic metal door that swung inward as we approached. Dr. Gregory ushered the crowd into a darkly lit passageway that was at least twenty yards wide, went on for hundreds of yards, and was lined with glass-walled cells on either side.

Wheeler addressed us when we reached the first compartment on the left, a blue chamber cut from stone and sealed by an extra-thick plate of glass.

"This man was dead and buried seven years ago," Wheeler said.

The prisoner was naked and in his mid-twenties. He was sitting on a stool, the only piece of furniture in the twenty-foot-wide room, and looking down at a spot between his feet.

"You have proof of this?" a woman with a German accent asked.

"There," Wheeler said, pointing at a small table standing outside the glass cage. "Those folders give all the information you will need to believe our claims. There are fingerprints and gene testing, retinal scans where they have been possible, and family and public photographs of the prisoners in life and in death."

The audience lined up to see the folders, but I stayed back. I didn't care what they said. I was worried about my sister and, at the same time, numbed by the notion that my father had possibly come back to life.

"What's so special about this prisoner, other than these documents?" a Spanish-sounding dark-skinned man asked.

"The atmosphere in that cell is fifty percent carbon monoxide," Wheeler said with a smirk.

"No."

"Arnold," Wheeler said to one of the soldier-aides. "Admit the bird."

The soldier went in through a door on one side of the blue cell and came out with a small cage that contained a gray dove. He went to the other side of the glass wall and opened a hatch in the stone. Placing the fluttering bird in the small space, he closed the tiny door and then pushed a button that opened a panel inside the cage, allowing the bird to enter. The dove took wing, crossed half the width of the room, and then fell dead before the naked man.

The prisoner picked up the little corpse and stared at it a moment. Then he looked up at me. He shook his head, dropped the dove, and returned his attention to the space between his bare feet.

"Carbon monoxide," a black man with a French accent said. "How is that possible?"

"These creatures are almost invulnerable to harm," Wheeler replied. "They bleed but don't die. They choke but don't expire. They are extraordinarily strong, and for all intents and purposes, they don't age."

"What are they?" the man asked.

"Demons from hell."

We visited forty-seven cages in all. There were male and female prisoners. Some in subzero environments, others in temperatures above anything a human could survive. One man was completely submerged in water, while others were in various forms of poisonous atmospheres. All of them were alive and conscious, but none spoke, unlike the child who had been slaughtered by the soldier.

The tour took over four hours. No one complained or asked to leave. I don't even remember anyone asking for a toilet, though someone must have.

I was sickened by the display. So far Wheeler hadn't proved the threat of these creatures. All he had shown was that they were superior and helpless. It was as if a bunch of apes had captured a heavenly host of angels and were torturing them for their beauty.

When we returned to the auditorium, the crowd was nearly silent.

"There you have it," David Wheeler announced from the dais. "You men and women represent nations and consortiums from around the globe. But more important, you are the last hope for humankind. If these creatures are allowed a foothold in our world, they will devour us."

"Where are they from?" a woman asked in a tremulous voice.

As if her question had been planned, the lights went down and the screen behind Wheeler lit up. An image appeared, containing a few dozen small amoeba-like creatures, each of which had triangular trunks surrounded by myriad waving tentacles. The organisms were swimming around in a clear liquid.

"These are the microorganisms that have been found in of all the prisoners," Wheeler said. "They are DNA-based, so we are sure that they are of earthly origin. But they are unlike any life-form now extant on the face of the planet. They are small but extraordinarily complex."

The image changed to a greater magnification, showing only a few of the organisms swimming together. They were beautiful. Scarlet and turquoise and sky blue flecked with silver and ebony and a deep forest green. One of the amoebas swam into another; they combined for a moment, creating a long abacus-like life-form that glimmered for a brief time. Then the amoebas flowed out of each other. This process was repeated six or seven times among the three beings, and then they flowed away from one another.

"They have all the appearance of the basis of animal life," Wheeler continued, "but the makeup of their basic DNA is much closer to that of bacteria."

"Impossible!" a man shouted.

"We thought so, too," Dr. Wheeler agreed. "But the evidence is irrefutable.

You are welcome, Dr. Hingis, to evaluate our studies for yourself."

"And where do you suppose such an impossible life-form emerged?" Dr. Hingis asked.

The image on the screen was replaced by a three-dimensional image of a planet, a huge globe that might have been the earth at one time. A small object was depicted moving toward the planet, and when it collided, a great cloud rose in the northern hemisphere of the gray and blue world. The image switched to a close-up of the depth of damage incurred.

"A billion years ago," Wheeler intoned, "more, a meteorite struck our planet and drove a significant portion of rudimentary life deep into the crust of the earth. There this life clung to existence. For eons it struggled against and then finally mastered its environment."

"How?" a woman asked.

"By developing a means of merging and measuring, of combining with its mates, of defining its surroundings and then altering structurally to survive. This was a very early form of life and not easily retarded by extreme temperatures or the lack of sun. These creatures learned to live on the minerals and elements of the earth."

The image began going through a series of different phases, all of them contained by the same globe. A purple cloud formed far below the surface, and as one image replaced the other, the cloud changed hue — growing sometimes larger, sometimes smaller — and began a slow migration toward the surface.

I remembered GT's explanation of the Wave and its movement toward his grave. I gave in completely then to the idea that he was, or at least had been, my father. While representatives of every major nation and corporation pondered the so-called threat to our species, I lamented my words to the man whom I had denied. I'd been given a second chance to have him in my life, and I'd turned away.

"The communal organism moved for millennia toward the surface of the planet —"

"You believe that this — this mass of microscopic creatures has intelligence?" Dr. Hingis asked.

"Not exactly," Wheeler replied. "These beings' existence has developed around an intense struggle for survival. You have seen how three XTs spend ninety-four seconds merging and sharing calculations. We have recorded images of millions of such transitions. The XT has developed the ideal society. An environment in which all experience is shared — physically. It wasn't until the colony had migrated to the DNA of simple creatures and maybe even the corpses of dead animals that they began to develop what we call intelligence. Their form of survival gave them the ability to digest the genome and to repeat it. This is life using the basic trait of life to merge with and dominate the environment."

The hush in the hall was almost maddening. Even I understood the ramifications of the scientist's claims. This new life-form, the XT, had the ability to *read* DNA and every other quantifiable thing about a human being. Thoughts, dreams, instincts, images, emotions — everything that made up life could be quantified and repeated.

If the XT was our enemy, we would be defenseless against it. It was too small to shoot, resistant to heat and cold, seemingly impervious to poison or lack of air. And if every cell knew everything — or even almost everything — that all other cells knew, then it was nearly immortal in a real way.

"You say colony," a woman said. "Singular. Do you believe that there is only one mass of this contagion?"

"It's likely," Dr. Gregory said, stepping up to the podium. "There may have been many such groups at first, but we believe they were all in the same area and that they ultimately either perished or merged. It would be improbable for them to be more widely dispersed because of the impediment of stone."

"What about reproduction, David?" someone asked even as the question was forming in my mind.

"A good question, Mr. Tron," the host replied. "Using the most advanced computer system in the world, the Japanese Nine-two, we have continuously observed twelve million individual cells for over seven months. In that time there have been only fourteen hundred and ninety-eight reproductions and nearly a thousand deaths."

"These beings can die?"

"So it seems, my friend." Again the screen changed images. Whoever was at the video controls had worked so closely with Gregory and Wheeler that he knew instinctively what to put up on the screen.

This new picture was a microphotographic image of one of the XTs. At first it was swimming along just fine, but then it began to vibrate. The tremors became more and more violent until finally the triangular head vaporized, leaving the tentacles to wilt into dust.

"What causes this demise?" Dr. Hingis asked.

"We believe," Dr. Wheeler said, "it has something to do with the atmosphere. Methane, ammonia, and alcohol. We've tried to reproduce the toxin, but our studies have so far proved fruitless.

"The reason we have called together this eminent body of scientists and ambassadors is therefore twofold. First, you must convince your governments that this threat is real and must be dealt with before it is too late. Second, you must take our studies and help us create the toxin to destroy this menace."

The discussion became more and more complex after that. Hingis and Tron and many other scientists started asking questions that I didn't understand. For a while everyone spoke in French and then in equations and calculations. Their communication was so technical that they seemed to me somewhat like the XTs they were so frightened of.

After another ten minutes, I got up and walked out of the auditorium.

I was met at the exit by the two soldiers who had driven me to the compound.

"Please come with us, Mr. Porter," the taller one said.

There was no option for me to refuse.

21

They showed me to a small apartment far removed from the scientific center and the seemingly endless number of cells for the XTs.

There was a bedroom, a toilet with a shower stall, and a combination kitchen–sitting room. The refrigerator contained a dozen eggs, a package of processed cheese slices, a pillowy loaf of white bread, some sliced ham, and a jar of grape jelly. In the cabinet was government-issue peanut butter, instant coffee, and a big bottle of nondairy creamer.

There were no books, no television, no radio. There was a desk next to my bed, which was only a cot. A desk drawer contained a ream of white typing paper and a yellow plastic disposable mechanical pencil. No more than five minutes after I entered into the apartment-cell, I began to write this history.

I wrote obsessively, putting down every experience, every word that I could remember. I had scrawled over the front and back of almost twenty sheets when some-body knocked. I hurriedly shoved the pages into the top drawer of the desk and said, "Yes?"

"May I come in, Mr. Porter?" David Wheeler asked pleasantly.

I opened the door and ushered my jailer into the room.

"Not much of a home, but you won't be here long," he said, looking around the bleak chamber. He sat on the small bed, and I settled back into my chair.

"It's illegal for you to hold me like this, against my will," I said.

"Not when it comes to Homeland Security," he said with an ironic smile.

"You can hardly call amoebas terrorists."

"What did she say to you?" he asked.

It might have seemed like a non sequitur, but I knew what he was talking about.

"Who?"

"That thing who called herself Mary-Beth. You know what I mean, Errol."

"No, David," I said. "No, I don't. She screamed and called us scum or something like that. But she didn't say anything to me specifically."

"She looked you in the eye."

"Maybe she could tell that I didn't want her to come to harm."

"Maybe. What were you writing?"

"Are you having me watched?"

"Every room in this facility is monitored, Errol," he said. "I'm sorry, but that's just the way it is. When you come to stay at my home, you'll have a bit more privacy."

"I'm not going anywhere with you."

Wheeler smiled. He held up his hands and hunched his shoulders, telling me that he understood but there was nothing that he or I could do about the situation.

In a flash, I understood the difference between human beings and the cellular life that made up the XTs' reanimations. There was no inflection for those tiny beasts. They merged, shared completely. Such communication was a kind of surrender that had no use for subterfuge or misdirection. All knowledge for the XT was concrete and complete. All intelligence was also instinct. How amazing it must have been for them to discover a life-form that used primitive gestures and sounds to communicate. How lonely we must have seemed in our separateness.

"I just came by to ask you about that look," David said. "Gregory wants to hold you for further study, but that's useless. We've already examined you, and there's no sign of any XT activity in your systems."

"Are they deadly?" I asked, worried about the wounds that had healed overnight.

"To living beings?" Wheeler asked rhetorically. "We don't know. Certain soldiers have volunteered for living XT cells to be introduced to their systems. So far the cells have remained separate from their internal biology. They are very brave men and women, knowing that if we are unable to remove the alien cells from their systems, they will have to be destroyed, along with the rest of the infestation, when we develop a toxin to kill them off."

"That doesn't sound very scientific, Doctor," I said. "I mean, don't you believe in the sanctity of life?"

"Yes, I do, Errol. But if I look up and see a tiger stalking me, the first thing I do is open fire. The most precious life is my own."

"But you have no proof that these organisms are stalking us."

"They are taking over the bodies of our dead, rising from the graves, and they're all but indestructible," he said very reasonably. "We must strike before we are destroyed by them."

I felt a thrill of fear while he spoke. After all, he was the expert, while I was just an unemployed computer programmer turned potter. Maybe the fate of humanity was at stake.

Maybe I shouldn't have lied to my captors.

Wheeler chose that moment to rise from the cot.

"I'll leave you now, Errol. You are invited to join me for breakfast in the morning."

He left before I could speak up. Maybe the future of the world would have been altered if he hadn't had somewhere to be just then.

Maybe.

I fell asleep at the desk writing. I knew that the pages would be confiscated, but there was no other way to occupy my time. I roused somewhere in the night and crawled into the bed, falling into a deep slumber. I don't know the time, because I didn't have a watch and there was no clock in my cell.

In my dreams, I was floating in the earth, moving through stone as if it were air. Sensations came from all around me: gravities and vibrations (not sounds) and other events that had no other correlation to my corporeal existence. I was immense, moving leisurely through solid stone at the rate of an inch a century. Time passed. Time stayed the same. But every micron was filled with the ecstasy of numbers and sameness and matchless difference. I was many and one. I was forever, remembering back before I was conceived, into the far reaches of the beginning. There was joy and the anticipation of a light of exquisite brightness waiting above.

And then there were small single-celled moments of life that began and ended but stayed the same. They moved so quickly through the soil and waters. They devoured and digested, multiplied and died. There was experience, separate and alone. And there was loneliness breaking upon stone.

The life-forms became more complex until one day I found myself a man. He had died, was killed (murdered), and was thrown into a deep pit. He made sounds rather than merging. He multiplied far faster than we could imagine. He moved through openness and had senses that amazed me. That was over 412,362 times around the firmament. His name was Veil, and he was the first man we became.

I fell back into stone, moving slowly upward, creeping toward — the sun?

22

The sun was shining on my face. I thought of GT lying out naked on his back, cold and alone and remembering more years than any other living being in the cosmos. Older than dirt. Older than God. Immortal despite my mortality. No wonder he had been so afraid those first days in the grave-yard.

"Good morning," a woman said.

I opened my eyes and realized that the sun was not part of the dream. The woman who had been working in the garden the day before was standing at the foot of a large four-poster bed.

I was under a thick down comforter.

"You were crying in your sleep," she said.

"Where am I?"

"Back at the house you left yesterday."

She was lovely and sad, wearing a button-down tan blouse and a tight black skirt. The hem came to her knees but flared, seeming like it wanted to ride up.

"David asked me to look in on you," she said.

"Dr. Wheeler?"

She smiled. "My husband."

"You're keeping me prisoner," I told her.

"What else is new?" She looked at me from behind those adorable freckles. "Breakfast is in half an hour."

"How did I get here?" I asked.

"They brought you in last night. You were unconscious. Nobody said so, but I think they might have drugged you."

She shrugged and began to turn away.

"What's your name?" I asked her back.

"Krista," she said. "Krista Arnet-Wheeler."

I found my clothes in the closet. They had been washed and pressed and hung from a wire hanger.

The breakfast room was like a finger jutting out into what was left of the orange grove. Instead of walls, it had light gray netting pulled tight from ceiling to floor. The long dining table was made from dark wood. At the farthest end, Krista Arnet-Wheeler and David Wheeler sat before a set of plates. A black woman was hovering around them, putting down dishes filled with various breakfast foods.

David stood up when he saw me. He gestured for me to come over. "Come have breakfast with us, Errol."

"Thanks." I couldn't think of anything else to say. Nor could I remember the last time I'd eaten.

I was ravenous.

Wheeler pulled out a chair for me.

It was a family-style breakfast. Scrambled eggs, French toast, fat pork sausage seasoned with thyme, fresh-squeezed orange juice.

The coal-black servant was tall and severe, ageless beyond sixty, and wearing a powder-blue dress that seemed somehow powerless on her.

"Thalia, this is Errol Porter," David Wheeler said. "He'll be staying with us for a while."

Thalia's eyes took me in. I don't think she meant to show contempt, it's just that she had an imperious mien.

"Your sister is out of the ICU," Krista said as I swallowed the first bite of egg.

It embarrassed me that I hadn't thought about my sister yet this morning.

"And her baby?"

"Fine," Krista said with a kindly smile. "She's still in an incubator, but the reports said that they expect her to survive."

"Coffee?" Thalia said. It was only a word, but there was Texas all through it.

"Thank you," I replied.

When she had left the finger-room, I asked David, "So am I a prisoner here?"

"Yes," he said without shame. "This house has a twenty-four-hour guard around it. If you are found trying to escape, you will be caught or killed."

Krista was looking down at her juice.

"You're kidding."

"I don't have a sense of humor. Do I, dear?" He reached out for Krista's hand and pressed it.

"No, he doesn't," she said, giving me a wan, humorless smile.

"The whole world is at stake, Errol. You and I, Krista and Thalia don't matter in that. We are all prisoners of war."

"What war?" I asked the slender scientist. "I didn't see anybody fighting you. Those prisoners were just sitting there — being tortured."

"You mistook those husks for human beings because that's how they present themselves," he said. "They might just as well become a bear or a bird. We apprehended an infected man and dog in downtown L.A. just a couple of weeks ago."

The radio news item came back to me.

"The man who pushed the policemen off the roof downtown?"

"Yes," Wheeler said, "a man who died thirteen years ago. His dog died the next day, and there was such a bond between them that the family got special permission to allow them to be buried together."

"GT never sounded like he wanted to hurt anyone," I said. "He talked about to-getherness."

"They're parasites, Errol. We are the hosts. That's the kind of togetherness he was talking about."

Krista stood up then.

"Excuse me," she said. "I have to go shopping."

As she left, Thalia returned with a chrome pitcher. She poured me a cup of coffee and asked, "Cream?"

"Just a touch," I said.

Wheeler waited for her to depart again before he went on. "The men and women who have risen from those graves are puppets. They're an infestation that will drive us into extinction. You and I cannot allow that to happen."

I got stuck on the word *extinction*. I thought that all death was a form of extinction; that all of a man's memories and beliefs, his loves and tactile sensations, were in some way like a singular species of life. The man dies, and all that he was is gone forever.

"GT remembered me," I said. "He felt for me; expressed love for me. He was aware of who he was."

"Like a corpse farting in the morgue," Wheeler said. "It gives you a start at first, but then you get used to it."

"Like that child screaming when you ordered her arm cut off?"

"Like that monster," he corrected. "Who, even now, is reconstituting in the basement of XT-1."

"Why am I here?" I asked.

"Because of what we're doing right now," he said. "Your personal demon, this GT as you call him, is the first XT to contact a family member. He's different. And we want to know why."

"How do you know that no others have called their families?" I asked. "For all you know, there could be dozens of men and women at home with their loved ones right now."

There was a flash of green from light reflecting in Wheeler's right eye. He smiled.

"This infestation has come in waves," he said. "The first ghouls were fairly mindless when they came out. Uncooked, as Dr.

Gregory says. That's why they were dis-covered so easily. They were picked up wandering senselessly from the graveyard. They had no ability to speak for many weeks. And even when they did manage to communicate, they uttered only single-syllable words."

Naked . . . cold . . . The words came back to me as if I were listening to them on the phone the first time GT called me.

"They were experiments," Wheeler con-tinued. "The first attempts at invasion. Later, the ghouls could speak almost upon their first appearance."

"How did you know about them?" I asked.

"They were picked up by the police, one by one," he said, "wandering naked in the neighborhood around Evermore. The first three appeared in a week's time. Their fin-gerprints were taken and a bright young detective thought it wise to inform the FBI. Our unit was formed soon after that."

"How long has this been going on?"

"Eighteen months."

"At Fox Hills?"

"Your father was the first host to rise from that cemetery. All of the other resurrections came from Evermore Cemetery. We were sure that the infection was located solely under that property. That's why we had no surveillance of Fox. Our resources haven't been deep enough to keep active watch on all the graveyards around Los Angeles, and up until your case, we hadn't thought it necessary. But we know that the ghouls have been getting more sophisticated. We also know that they were all headed north. We thought we'd caught all of them until your father showed up."

"Nobody else called their families?" I asked.

"Not until you."

"How do you know?" I said. "A hundred XTs could have arisen there before my father."

Wheeler smiled and nodded. A sparrow flew up and grabbed onto the gray netting and then flew off again.

"The XTs leave certain evidence of their passage," the doctor said.

I remembered the cool soil in the grass covering my father's grave.

"Your father," Wheeler continued, "was in the only affected area at Fox."

I felt like an ant in a beetle's sand trap. Every step I took brought me closer to the chattering jaws of the predator. Even if I stayed still, holding my breath, the ground beneath me slowly gave way.

Wheeler sounded reasonable. But then I remembered how he'd ordered the severing of MaryBeth Coulder's arm. GT had all of the memories and at least believed he was my father. My father had killed a man in our living room and buried him in the garage. I had been kidnapped. My government was in a secret war. My rights as an American citizen were of no consequence. Every step, every detail of my life, seemed to be dragging me down.

The story my grandmother told about my cousin the arsonist came to mind. Albert Trellmore committed crimes against his enemies based on his own judgment. And when he judged himself guilty, he went to his bed and died.

"Tell me something, David," I said.

"What's that?"

"What kind of doctor are you?"

It seemed to me the most important question in the world. How Wheeler answered would determine my response to him. No president or senator or judge had called on me to protect humanity. This man, this doctor, had done so.

"I'm a general in the United States Army," he said.

"I didn't ask you about your rank," I

said. "You're a doctor, and I want to know what kind."

For the first time since we'd met, David Wheeler faltered. He laced his fingers, and a furrow came into his brow.

"I'm a plastic surgeon."

23

"Plastic surgeons are important physicians in the armed services," David Wheeler was telling me. "There are hundreds of thousands of soldiers in active service, and then there are the insured veterans. Reconstructive surgery due to disfigurement or physical dysfunction would be astronomical if we farmed out that work to the private sector."

I heard him, but I didn't care. I wasn't going to work in the service of a beauty doctor. I would make up my own mind, like my dead cousin the arsonist had done.

"And how did you become a general?" I asked, not really caring about the answer.

"Leadership comes in all professions," he said. "I became the youngest commander of a military hospital fifteen years ago. I haven't practiced in over a decade, but I don't have to be a surgeon to cut out this contagion."

We talked awhile longer. When breakfast was done, I told the general I was tired, that the experiences of the past few days had exhausted me. He said we'd meet for lunch and resume our talks then.

I asked him could I call my sister, but he said there was an order of silence imposed on the whole XT project and that no one who had been to the facility could have unsupervised contact with the outside world.

When I got back to the room, the pages I had written were there on my freshly made bed. There were also four long yellow legal pads, three yellow pencils, and a child's red plastic sharpener. I wondered who had left these items for me. Dr. Wheeler had probably brought them home, but he hadn't made the bed. And I doubted that he would have provided those particular writing utensils.

But right then I didn't care where the writing tools had come from. I threw myself into a diatribe against the government and the general in particular. I must have written thirty pages railing against my captors, but those words didn't make it into this history.

I realized that my anger meant nothing to the world. I was well fed and free to roam the house, at least. My movements were limited, but I wasn't in a jail cell. My sister and her child had survived, and no one would miss me except Angelique and my mom, and maybe Nella.

It was near to one o'clock when I realized the pettiness of my harangue. For a while I contemplated escape. I thought maybe I'd use my paper for plotting strategy. But then I worried there might be cameras located throughout the house, as there had been in the bunker. Even if Wheeler hadn't given me the paper, he might still be aware of it. And if I wrote down my plans, he could foil any effort.

So I went back to detailing the events as they had unfolded. The objective relating of facts would make Wheeler and his crew believe that I was controllable.

Not long after I had reached this determination, there came a soft knock at my door. It was the servant Thalia summoning me for lunch.

I met with Dr. Wheeler for the next four hours. I never lied to him once. I told him about the phone calls, about my mother's infidelities, and about the love GT seemed to have for my sister and me. I told him about GT's hunger and need to eat sand. That was the only time the good doctor took notes.

"Do you know what eating sand is all about?" I asked Wheeler.

"They eat quartz-based soil or pebbles, sand, as food. The insides of their stomach linings allow for the invading cells to come feast on the material."

"But if they need to eat, couldn't you starve them?" I asked.

"They don't die, they just go into hibernation," he said. "And if any quartz material is brought within their reach, they awaken and gorge."

He asked me many more questions, and I answered every one with complete candor. But I never mentioned GT's lyric mouthings about the Wave or his *mission*.

"Did any of them show violent tendencies against humans or other forms of life?" I asked at one point.

"The man who fought the police threw them from the roof," he said.

"But they attacked him first. What I want to know is if any of these people —"

"Creatures," he corrected.

"— if any of them actually attacked anyone without provocation."

"Not directly," he said. "But the beavers of North America didn't have to be aggressive to force out any species that couldn't live in harmony with their watery world. These XTs could very easily create environments that would be extremely unfriendly to human and mammal alike."

I told him that GT didn't have a scar that my father was marked with as a child.

"Of course not," he said. "GT, as you call him, is not your father. He's a simulacrum of the genetic code that once made up your father — not the man himself, not the physical experiences that made up your father."

"Then why does he have my father's memories?"

"Because the cells got to your father's brain before it had decomposed. Somehow the XT cell can reconstitute what it finds. Memories, mental functions, language, even the ability to learn."

I thought about how GT had said the cells counted the components of whatever structure they encountered. I thought about *count* in the word *encounter*. But I didn't share any of that with Wheeler. I had no reason to help him kill GT, and no reason had been proffered. Maybe these so-called XTs were my enemy. But I'd have to see that for myself before I'd help kill the man who thought I was his son.

I went back to my room and wrote down every word of our conversation as far as I could remember. I did this because I believed that our lunchtime talk had actually been an interrogation, that Wheeler would come back to the same questions some time later to see if my story was consistent. If I wrote down everything we said after each meeting, then I could keep on top of any inconsistencies that might arise.

I finished my notes at about nine that evening, took off my clothes, and got under the covers. I wasn't tired. My mind was racing back and forth over all the experiences I'd had since the first night GT had called.

While I was thinking, the door opened. Wheeler's wife walked in and sat next to me on the bed. She reached over me to turn on the lamp that sat on the side table next to my head. She was wearing a robe that hung open a bit. She was a well-endowed woman, and quite lovely.

"Are you awake?" she asked.

"You see my eyes open, don't you?"

She smiled and put her hand on my thigh through the blanket.

"We're all prisoners here," she said.

"Even David?"

"In his own way. David is obsessed with these resurrections. He's become like some crazy saint from the Middle Ages, out on a quest to destroy Satan in the world. They wouldn't let him quit even if he wanted to. But he doesn't want to."

"Are you the one who brought me my journal?" I asked.

"Yes. David had it in a briefcase. I thought you'd want to have it and to keep on writing. You have to have something to keep you sane in this prison."

"He won't let you leave?" I asked.

"No. Thalia and I are both prisoners. If we go shopping, we have a guard ride with us. Otherwise we are never allowed away from the house."

"Doesn't that sound odd?" I asked. "I mean, why keep everything such a secret? And even if you did talk to somebody, who's going to believe that there are zombies crawling up out of the grave?"

That's when she kissed me.

She lunged at my lips and shoved her luscious tongue almost down my throat. It was a muscular tongue. I was thinking about that when her hand went under the cover and grabbed the erection that had formed almost immediately.

"I need this," she said. "I need it."

I did, too. While she kissed me, I pulled off her robe. We were together in under a minute. We reached climax in half that time. But that didn't even slow down our lovemaking. She was on top of me, and then I was on top of her. With all of that rolling around, we were bound to fall off the bed. When we finally did, the impact of our bodies made a large booming sound.

"Maybe you should go," I said.

"With you this excited? I want to see your face when you come again. You look like a woman when you surrender to me."

"But somebody might hear us."

"Only Thalia, and she won't tell. David is at the facility. He won't be back until breakfast."

She slapped me then, hard across the face, and said, "Now shut up and fuck me."

24

The next month went along like that. The days I spent talking with Wheeler about GT and his odd ways. The doctor-general didn't share much with me about the goings-on in the government study. But now and then he let some information slip.

Like once when he said that many of the XTs in custody were aware of their families but didn't seem to have any more closeness with them than to any other human.

"They say things like 'This body's sire-side,'" Wheeler confided, "or 'The children of this one's womb.'"

GT was the only XT they knew of that had exhibited feelings for relations. Wheeler and his superiors worried that this was a kind of alien propaganda; that if these ghouls (his word, not mine) could lobby among the living, then they might start some movement that would retard the necessary actions needed to exterminate all XT cellular life.

Much of the time I spent at the Wheeler home, I felt as if I were going crazy. The nights I spent alone, I obsessed over many large and small matters. I worried about what Nella must have thought when she came back to the booth and found me gone. I worried about my mother and her grief over being the cause of her lover's murder. Krista gave me regular updates on my sister's health, but I didn't know whether to believe her.

It seemed ridiculous that I could walk freely around the two-story mansion but I could not walk away or even make a telephone call. I thought of pulling a knife on Wheeler or setting the house on fire, but I didn't have the physical courage to do either.

I spent much of the time writing. By then I realized that I probably wasn't being spied upon. Wheeler knew I was his prisoner and that he had complete control over my communication with the outside world, so he didn't feel the need to spy on me. I began this history in earnest. When I was at work on it, I felt that I was at least attempting to counter the insane and illegal activities of Wheeler and my government.

Three times a week, coinciding with Wheeler's scheduled "graveyard" shifts at the facility, I had wild sex with Krista, who said that she hadn't seen her husband with an erection in over a year and a half. She was lonely and starved for love. Every night he was gone, she'd come to my room, and I was always ready for her. Some evenings we got a little rough with each other. She was the stronger of us, so any wrestling ended up with her on top. And if I happened to win, she would slap me and push me to the floor.

Even now, when I remember that month, I get aroused.

I was also morally conflicted, wondering if I should be answering more of David's questions. Maybe he was right. Maybe the fate of mankind really was at stake. But his unshakable intention to commit genocide on the life-form that had resuscitated my father always stopped me short. The tension that arose in me was eased by sex with my captor's wife.

"Do you love me?" she asked one night, about two weeks after we'd been having sex.

I did not, but I said, "Yes. I love you."
"You do?"

"Yes, I do. You know I haven't even been able to make love with a woman since my wife left me."

I hadn't told Krista about Nella. I felt guilty being with another woman since Nella and I had been together, and I didn't want Krista asking me questions about her.

"Really?" Krista asked. "Why not?"

"It's just that you make me feel more comfortable. I feel that I can be a man with you."

Men and women, I think, know intrinsically how to lie to each other. I needed Krista on my side, so I gave her the power over me with my words.

She didn't talk about leaving her husband or going off with me. All she needed was for me to tell her that she was the only woman who could have my heart. In turn, she told me that I was the best and sweetest she had ever known.

I waited for another week to pass before suggesting that we escape.

"Then we could be together," I said.

I may have even believed it at the time. The little I'd had in life was gone. I hadn't paid my rent, so Felicity Fine had probably moved me out of the garage. Nella had the money I'd taken from Bobby Bliss's grave, but who knew what she'd do with that after I had walked out on her without a word? And even if Nella kept my money, she'd probably move on to another man. Why wouldn't she? None of that mattered, because I'd never see her again anyway. The government would be after me if I escaped. I could never go back to the life I'd known.

"No," Krista said. "I can't go. I'm too old to be on the run. And you should stick it out. Why put your life on the line when they may come up with the toxin any day? Scientists around the world are working on it now. Once they come up with the right cocktail, the reason for secrecy will be over."

"Do you think it's right to exterminate the XTs?" I asked.

"I don't know," she said. "David says it's like any other disease, that it needs to be stopped before it infects the whole world."

"But how can that be?" I asked my secret lover. "The way they see it, the whole being multiplies less than a fraction of a fraction of a percent in a year. There couldn't be much of an invasion if the disease doesn't reproduce."

"Maybe there's already enough in the ground to overtake us," Krista said, parroting her husband. "Like oil or natural gas."

"I don't know," I said. "But I'd sure like to get away from here."

"Stay awhile longer," she said, kissing me tenderly.

At some point in the middle of the night, I came to the realization that Krista had no more intention of letting me go than did her husband.

That was when I decided to try and escape without her help.

I had already made a tentative plan. I'd make it out by hiding in the SUV on one of the outings that Thalia or Krista took. I didn't know if there were sentries that searched them on the way out. But I reasoned that guards at the gate would arouse suspicion among the neighbors.

The other problem was surveillance. I had no idea if there were cameras set up at the various access points of the house. They could have cameras anywhere.

One night I decided I had to try to escape. Even if I failed, I would at least know what kind of system they were using. I couldn't just stay in my room waiting for Wheeler to decide on my fate.

The next day, I found a large blanket in a hall closet and carried it to my room. Just as I was closing my door, I saw Thalia watching from down the hall.

I tried to think of something to say, but there was nothing. Thalia and I never spoke. I had tried to talk to her those first few days, figuring that the old-time bond between blacks that had grown up through the racism of America would put us on the same side in the struggle against white Wheeler. But she never shared a personal moment with me. All she ever uttered was *yes* and *no* or *Dr. Wheeler said . . .*

I was going to use the blanket to hide under. Maybe nobody would look. Maybe if they did look, the blanket wouldn't arouse suspicion.

I knew Krista planned to go shopping the next day, because she had said so at lunch. I was ready to go. The government couldn't come after me with all their force, because the XT project was still top-secret. I'd go south and then east. I'd change my name and wait for a sign that the government was through with their machinations.

It wasn't much of a plan.

It didn't really make sense.

Why run if I was in a nice home with food and a television set, a bed to sleep in, and sex three times a week? Where would I end up? Why go?

By three in the morning, I had decided against escape. Krista was right. I'd stay.

Not long after that, the door came open. I switched on the lamp. David was home that evening, so I was surprised to see Krista.

"Turn it off," she said.

She sat on the bed, but there was no leaning over me in heat as she usually did. She was quiet and still.

"Errol."

"What?"

"Dr. Gregory has been running tests on your blood ever since you left XT-1," she said in a rush. "He's found an abnormality and has gotten permission from higher up to have you brought in for more tests. David says that you're to be taken away day after tomorrow."

"For how long?"

She didn't respond.

"How long, Krista?"

"He said that you very well may not be coming back."

My tongue went completely dry. I started coughing. I reached for the water pitcher next to my bed and drank straight from it without bothering about the glass. But no matter how much I drank, the thirst could not be quenched.

Krista sat in the gloom of the dark room like Wheeler's angel come to proclaim my death.

"What does it mean?" I asked.

"They may reclassify you as an XT," she said.

"No."

"You have to escape," my lover said with conviction.

I told her my plan, and she said that it might work. Tomorrow it was just her and Jerome the guard going off together. She said that I should wait after breakfast and then go down to the garage and climb in the back and get under my blanket.

"Don't make a sound," she said. "And remember that I love you. And that I'm sorry. I'm very sorry about having to put you through this."

I thought at the time that she meant the threat of annihilation at the hands of her husband's masters.

25

Breakfast was as always. Wheeler engaged me in subtle interrogation while Thalia served and Krista interrupted now and then to talk about her house duties and the progress of her gardens.

"Have you checked on the plant life around the graveyards?" I asked Wheeler at one point.

"What do you mean?" he asked.

"The trees. Don't you think the XTs might want to inhabit the trees? I mean, they did that dog."

"Is this anything that your GT suggested?"

"No. No. He never talked about plants. I just thought that might be something you would have checked."

"That's helpful, Errol. I'm pleasantly surprised."

"I'd like to be of help," I said. "I mean, if these cells are as dangerous as you say, we'll all have to fight them."

Wheeler stared at me, his dense green eyes reflecting the diffuse light of the orchard.

"Dr. Gregory thinks our talks have been fruitless. He says that he's not interested in the psychology of the XT but in their instinctual drive. He tells me that I'm wasting valuable research time on you."

"No, sir," I said, thinking that I'd gone too far with *sir*.

"Well," Wheeler said, "tomorrow you and I will take a drive down to XT-1 and speak to Gregory personally about your newfound patriotism."

The garage was attached, and the door connecting it to the house was unguarded and unlocked. Krista had given me the extra remote to unlock the car doors. The side lights flashed, and the beep of the horn sounded to me like a sonic boom, but no one came. I burrowed under the gray-blue blanket and waited for my chance at freedom.

I told Wheeler that I'd sat up all night worrying about my lack of enthusiasm in our talks. I was eager to help, but I should probably get some sleep. I begged off on our late-morning meeting, knowing that if I hesitated, Dr. Gregory would have me on an autopsy table before the week was out.

I don't know that I fell asleep there waiting for Krista and Jerome, but I did have a vision that I thought was a dream.

There was a place far away and in darkness but not in the earth. It was cold and unfriendly, silent except for the weak reminiscence of gravity and light. There was a song, or maybe just a note or two, playing in the distance. It was a language used by beings now dead and gone. But the words they spoke were their salvation. They had become their language and were now looking for someone to hear them and speak their name. Their voices traveled the universe waiting for a receiver, for the chance to breathe again.

Another voice drowned out this sibilant whisper. It was the deep and robust song of a far-traveler passing nearby. It was the radiant opera of an infinite, intangible entity that had occurred only once, in absolute perfection; a unitude of perfectly balanced ideas that was now seeking to breathe its life into another.

Then there was a long sermon on the perpetuity of vibrations and sunlight in an endless field of quartz. This oration had something to do with the changing of Law depending upon placement in the physical universe. There was a high moral stance to the lecture and there were many dissenting views, but I didn't really understand much of it. I didn't know where I was or who was speaking. I didn't know which sense organs perceived these communiqués or what language was being spoken. But it was all one tongue, I was sure of that.

One tongue in an endlessly varied cosmic patois.

The doors of the car opened and slammed shut.

"How long will we be gone?" the guard Jerome asked.

"As long as it takes," Krista replied.

The words were rude, but her tone was friendly enough.

The ignition turned over. I heard the echo of that universal language in the lurching engine. The garage door was engaged. The car started moving. My heart was beating so hard that I held my breath to slow it down.

While they drove, Krista and Jerome talked. She was in the backseat, nearer me, but I couldn't make out what either of them was saying. After maybe twenty minutes, we still seemed to be on dirt roads, which was odd, because, as I remembered it, the paved highway was only about ten minutes from Wheeler's door.

The car came to a stop, and one of the doors opened. When I heard Jerome's army boots crunching gravel, I knew I had been found out somehow. Maybe Krista had betrayed me. Why? I felt around for something to defend myself with.

The back door opened.

"Not today, Jerry," Krista said.

A zipper sounded.

There was a grunt and then a moan.

"I need it, baby," he said.

There was about five minutes of kissing and whispers. Krista stopped telling him no.

The SUV started rocking, and they talked to each other. Krista groaned in pleasures that I hadn't known it was possible for her to achieve. I realized that I was only one of her lovers, only a part of her despair over Wheeler and his remote war.

At one point Krista was screaming. Jerome was urging her on in a voice much lower than he usually used. We were all swaying together. Despite my feeling of abandonment, I had an erection. Then they stopped. If they had gone on much longer, I might have climaxed with them.

"I love you," Jerome said tenderly.

Krista said something, but I couldn't make it out. It was a whisper of love. I knew she was trying to protect me from hearing her tell another man the words we had shared.

Jerome got back into the driver's seat and started the engine. He drove for what seemed a very long time.

We slowed and then moved in tight circles for a while. The car stopped, and both the front and back doors came open. The horn beeped. The locks clicked into place.

"I want to buy chocolate, Jerry," Krista said in a happy voice.

That was the last time I ever heard Krista Arnet-Wheeler's voice. And even though she was walking off with another man, I couldn't be angry. She had saved my life. She had done more than anyone else had ever done for me — risked her own safety without a moment's hesitation.

26

Climbing out of the SUV, I found myself at the Beverly Center shopping mall, feeling like an escaped convict but not looking the part. Two weeks before, Krista had bought me a pair of gray cotton slacks and a primarily yellow Hawaiian shirt. She'd put a small leather shoulder bag under the backseat. It contained my wallet, with two hundred dollars in small bills, and a hefty bagged lunch. I had also brought the five-hundred-plus sheets of my memoir.

I walked out of the center and headed for Santa Monica Boulevard. From there I went west until I reached Beverly Hills. There's a slender park along the north side of the boulevard that goes on for miles. I sat down on a park bench and ate my salami and cheese sandwich and pondered my hopeless predicament.

Two hundred dollars could buy me a bus ticket somewhere. But where? What would I do when I got there? And what about what I knew?

Krista had taken a chance on me. Maybe

I should take a chance. Maybe Wheeler could be beaten.

Halfway through my banana, I decided to stay in L.A. for at least a few days. After eating, I went into the public library and set myself up on the computer. I logged on using my I.D., thinking that the government might not be after me quite yet. I was hoping to find everything I could about Wheeler and Gregory and the term *XT*.

I never got that far.

Hi.

The instant messenger was Shellyshell11. I couldn't have thought of a better person to talk to right then. I answered immediately.

Hi, honey. I know you probably just wanted to say hey but I've got some serious problems right now and I could really use some help.

Sure, Err. I'm at my mom's new house. She's in Laurel Canyon. On Natterly.

She gave me the address, and I logged off. I remembered then that she had said she was coming to L.A. The thought that I could be with someone I knew exhilarated me. Someone who wasn't crazy. Someone who cared about me, even if only as a soon-to-be-ex-husband.

I called a taxi. It took quite a while to find her place, since the streets of Laurel Canyon are based on mountain paths originally set down by erosion. There was no sense to them, so it cost forty-two dollars to make it to her house.

"Hey, Err," Shelly said at the front door of the modest-looking home.

There she was. Mocha skin with straightened bleached-blond hair. She had the most voluptuous figure in high school, but back then she wore loose clothes to hide it. Now her flimsy coral blouse and tight ocher skirt showed off every curve.

She kissed me. Then she kissed me again.

"I've missed you, boy," she said.

I wondered briefly if *boy* was an endearment she used for Thomas. But I didn't have the luxury of jealousy. There were men out there who wanted to cut me just to see if I might die.

"I need your help, Shell," I said.

"Sure, Err."

Her smile turned into concern, and she stepped aside so I could come in.

The house was actually a mansion. The body of it was down in a valley behind the facade, which was like the eyes of a crocodile that broke the surface but whose body lay below. Four steps down, we entered into a basketball court used as a living room.

"This is your mom's house?" I asked, forgetting my worries for a moment.

"She married this rich guy after my father died —"

"Your father died?"

"Over a year ago. Mom wanted to tell you, but things were so new with me and Tommy, and he came out, so —"

"What did he die of?" I asked, ignoring her indelicate explanation.

"Heart attack. He was on the stationary bike." Shelly's voice broke, and I put my arms around her.

It was an instinctual move. I thought about the XTs, how they blended together when they came into proximity.

She cried, and I wondered what Gregory had found in my blood. I wondered where GT was. The image of the bone-dry corpse in my parents' garage appeared before my eyes, and I cried along with my soon-to-be-ex-wife.

The doorbell rang.

I gasped so violently that my windpipe clenched, sending a pain down into my chest.

"Don't answer it," I said.

"Why not?"

"Because there're people after me. They want to take me away."

"What people?" Shelly asked. "Why?"

"It's a long story, honey. But you got to believe that I need to hide from them."

"Get into that closet," she said, gesturing toward an oak-stained pine door. "I'll send them away."

"Don't tell them that you heard from me. Don't tell them anything."

The closet was empty and smelled from varnish. I supposed that Mrs. Larman and her new husband had just moved. I strained to hear any word, but the front door was half a court away. I squatted there with my ear pressed to the wood until it came open. Shelly loomed above me.

"Who was it?" I asked.

"He said that his name was GT," she said. "He said that he followed you here on a bicycle. I'm going to call the police."

"No!" I grabbed Shelly by the ankle.

"Ow!"

"Please, baby. Let me handle this. GT isn't the one after me. They're after him, too."

"Why was he following you?"

I didn't know the answer to that question, so I went to the front door and opened it. He was standing there, patiently waiting for me.

He had on black trousers that fit him, and a long-sleeved white dress shirt with the tails out and the cuffs unbuttoned. His mane of matted hair had been cut down to an acceptable length. He was smiling, and I couldn't hold back from hugging him.

"Dad."

"So what is it you're telling me?" Shelly was asking me.

Her mother and her new husband, Rinaldo Smith, were in Baja California on a camping trip with a group of seniors. The kitchen, where we were standing, looked onto bare hillsides leading down into the valley.

I was drinking coffee. Shelly looked to me for the answers, but now and then she'd cut frightened stares at GT. When we were just kids, she and my father were close, so GT's manners and ways with her

196

were unsettling. She could see the man inside the boy.

We tried to explain everything, GT in his way and me in mine.

"I don't know," I said. "The government guys think that GT is inhabited by a virus or something that wants to infect the entire world."

"Are you contagious?" Shelly asked the boy.

"Only if I want to be," he said with a smile. "And I'd have to want to, really bad."

"Did you cure my fingers?" I asked him.

"They were infected, and I wanted you to see what I saw so that you could know me."

"So I have those XT things in me?"

"The Wave, Airy," he corrected. "Far beyond anything you've ever known or seen or believed was possible. But now you have seen it. I can tell that you have. You've been floating in the granite, passing through stone toward the chorus of the infinite."

"What is he talking about, Errol?" Shelly asked.

It was too large to explain by just talking. "I don't know. I really don't. Somehow GT here is related to my old man. He knows things and he can do things. That's why the government is after him. All I can tell you is that I saw them murder a girl who was like him. They cut her to pieces for no reason at all."

"What are you talking about?" Shelly asked. "The government murdered a child?"

"I saw it with my own eyes."

"I can't believe that," she said.

It was true. I saw in her face that she couldn't accept what we were telling her. There was a web of worry-wrinkles between her eyes. For a few more hours, she'd listen and try to believe, but sooner or later, she would have to pull away. We were obviously crazy, and she had never disobeyed the law in her life.

Realizing this, I said, "Shelly, we have to go. I don't want you to tell anyone that we've been here. I mean, don't tell them unless they threaten you. Then tell them everything."

"Where will you go?" she asked, sounding a little relieved. "You can't just run from the government."

"It's either that or die," I said.

"The government wouldn't kill an innocent person."

"They'd slaughter all of Los Angeles to keep GT and his kind from seeing another sunrise."

27

At GT's request, Shelly drove us up into the Malibu Hills in her mother's new Lexus. Standing at the foot of a dirt path, I kissed her good-bye.

"When are you going to come back?" she asked me.

"Soon, I hope."

"Oh, Errol."

Shelly loved me at that moment. On the ride down, she had talked about her and Thomas. It was the only time she had to tell me about her life. They were having a trial separation. She wanted to get away and see what she was like on her own. They'd probably get back together, she said. But she loved me right then at the foot of that nameless dirt road. I was sure of that.

GT led me into the hills, heading north and east. We traversed the rough and rocky terrain at my pace, because GT didn't get tired. We scuttled over big stones and through dense brush. Every now and then we came to a street or dirt road, but for the most part, we were outside the range of man-built structures. We ascended into sparse forest and then into thicker woodlands. A few times we crossed cultivated rows of farm acreage. GT was following a path that might have been paved and inlaid with gold. He never seemed to wonder where he was going.

He talked to me about things I had done as a child. He said that my mother and he would worry because sometimes I would forget to breathe.

"You mean hold my breath?" I asked him.

"No," he said. "You'd just be sitting there not breathing. Maddie would say, 'Are you breathing, Errol?' and you would inhale and say, 'I am now, Mama.' Damnedest thing."

When he spoke like that, he was an exact replica of my father. It broke my heart with yearning at first, and then it made me mad. He wasn't my real father. My father was an old man who had died of cancer, who never would have been leading me through the wilderness to escape hostile government agents.

"What are you?" I asked him.

"You know," he said.

I felt a flash in my mind, and I saw the XT creatures again. This time they weren't on a microscope slide but floating all around me. They moved gracefully, gesturing with their long tentacles, which had small protuberances like fingers all around their tapered tips.

A tentacle's hand reached out for me, seeking a gentle touch, it seemed. But the "hand" broke through my skin and went deep into my chest. The pain was extraordinary. I made to yell, but one of the tentacles jammed itself down my throat. The appendages entered my spine and thigh; one came up under my left sole, while still another entered my rectum. Inside me the alien arms expanded, inflating my body until I was sure that I'd explode.

Then there was a pop. Suddenly I was fully inflated like a huge human balloon. I was the size of the hill we were ascending.

Even though I was under the spell of the powerful hallucination, I was also aware of moving along with GT, climbing toward a wooded mountaintop.

Inside me, things were happening. The fingertips connected to nerve clusters. Pulsing energy began to chatter throughout my body. These pulses were counts that added up — I don't know how — to ideas not unlike the communiqués in my day-dream under the blanket in Wheeler's SUV.

Unity was a recurring theme. Onetwothree was another concept, a triangular form that interconnected in all directions, a three-dimensional counting system that somehow moved forward and backward through time.

I knew things that I had known when I was five and six and seventeen but that I had forgotten later on.

I was a three-year-old standing in front of my mother, looking up at her cranberry-colored housedress. While she was telling me that I was bad, bright forms of the XTs floated around her head.

I glanced to my right and saw that GT and I were coming to the top of a rise. Before us stretched a forested valley that led to another mountain. How long had I been in the dream?

When I turned back, I was six and on a fishing barge with my father. He was teaching me to gut mackerel. I grabbed a ten-inch fish with my left hand, holding the knife awkwardly with my right. I tried to press the point of the blade into the white underbelly, but the mackerel writhed and bucked. It leaped from my grasp and fell to the deck. At that moment I stared into its eye, where I saw my reflection. Then I was the fish looking out at me. I twisted my sleek body and fell through an opening under the guard wall.

I fell into the water and swam down quickly.

Moving through the cold Pacific elated me. But there was something missing. I went deeper and then up toward the light, along the surface and then down again.

Far off there was a cloudy, undefined figure emerging from the murky deep. As it moved closer, I held my breath and flipped my tail. And then I was in the cloud, one of many hundreds of fish like me. I was me and all around me, elated and strong.

I turned away from the school and found myself looking at a black computer screen filled with hexadecimal symbols.

Math, I thought. It's all numbers.

By that time the mackerel was trapped in the beak of a snow-white seagull, being carried to an island beach.

It was nighttime, and GT and I were still walking. I was staggering but without complaint. I wasn't walking through a eucalyptus forest at midnight but soaring at midday, a seagull gliding with fourteen other birds like me.

The ocean spread out forever, and the sky beat against our feathered wings, making a music that I loved more than flight itself.

"GT," I gasped.

I was now a larva burrowing into the flesh of the dead seabird.

"What, Airy?"

"I can't stop seeing these things. It's driving me crazy."

"Then stop doing it," he said, and the visions ceased.

I fell to my knees and took a deep breath. When I looked up, I saw the sun rising over a mountain crest. The light was like God on the first day and I was a firmament. Then things went black.

When I opened my eyes again, the air was very cold. The sun shone brightly, but my feet and hands hurt from the chill. GT squatted next to me, looking into my face.

"You awake?" he asked, once again mimicking the man whose genes he wore.

"It's cold."

"I've called for help."

"What kind of help?"

"You'll see," he said, and I lost consciousness again.

When I awoke the second time, I was warm, though the night air was freezing. All around me were coarse furry bodies, each one like a furnace. They smelled of wild animal, feral and sharp. Mixed in among the hot bodies was GT. I caught a glimpse of his face. His eyes were closed, but then they opened, revealing dark spaces that reflected the crowd of stars above us.

The next time I opened my eyes, the russet-colored, prehistoric wolves that had warmed me were milling around a mountain crest. GT was down on all fours with them, licking up dirt from the ground.

When I came up to them, he got to his feet, rubbing the gravelly dirt from his chin.

"Dirt is your food?"

"Sand and sun," he said. "Sand and sun."

"Where are we?" I asked my father, the alien guide.

One of the wolves howled.

"Near the cave," he said. "Cave of the Wave."

"How far did I walk?"

"Twenty miles, maybe twenty-five. What it took the Wave ten million years to pass. And then I carried you for a long time."

"Are they after us?"

"Oh yes," he said. "They have been passing over this place with airplanes and helicopters for months now. They look, but they do not find. They rummage around in and among the trees, but they are blind to what we are and where."

One of the wolves rubbed up against me. She was warm, and I knelt to embrace her for the heat.

"Do you remember when I took you horseback riding, Airy?"

When I just listened to his voice, I knew that he was my father. The pang of that realization, along with one of my fondest memories, made my chest rise.

"Yes."

"That was nothing next to what you will soon see."

28

The beasts that accompanied us were giants compared to any wolf I had ever heard of. They must have weighed six hundred pounds each. Their snouts were unusually long.

"Why wolves and men?" I asked my father.

"The Wave has flowed into many of our distant cousins," he said, his grin filled with primordial joy. "Butterflies and locusts, house cats and weeds. But it was man, we knew, who would fear us and strike out. We took human form because that has always been our defense."

"To become your enemy?"

"To be him."

"So Wheeler was right," I said. "You are our enemy."

"No, Airy. No. We offer a greater vision, a world without division. Hope."

"You defend yourself by offering hope?"

GT grinned and clapped me on the shoulder. A huge wolf tongue licked my left hand.

Under the cover of a pine forest, we traveled — one man, eight extinct wolves, and the resurrected corpse of my father.

"Where are we going?" I asked GT at midmorning.

"The Wave."

"Where's that?"

"Up yonder, boy." His words had been spoken in a western we'd watched together on late-night TV when I was nine.

For years I had prayed to see him one more time, and now that we were together, I hadn't told him how I felt.

"I love you, Dad."

GT and the wolves stopped. They all turned to regard me. Actually, only GT gazed at me. The wolves began to circle us, coughing and barking as that species of wolf must have done for millennia before man had risen upright.

"Love me?" he said.

"Yeah. I missed you for all those years, and now you're back. I mean, it's crazy, and you're not quite right, but you are my father, I know that. And I've missed you every day since the day you died."

"Death," GT said. "Me. You. These are things we never knew in the old times, in the deep earth. There was only us and then the voices."

"What are those voices?" I asked.

"Have you heard them?"

"In my head. Like faraway proclamations or sermons or calls."

"They are in the sky," GT said. "In space. There are more voices than there are stars. But there is only One that comes."

"What is it?"

"The Annunciation," he said with a sly smile.

We walked all day. At night, three of our six wolf companions went off. They came back bearing trout in their jaws. I knew how to rub two sticks together. I made a fire to cook the catch. I hadn't eaten in a long time. Those fish tasted better than anything I'd ever eaten.

We hadn't gone very far in the morning when we came to a mountainside cave. Our crew entered the cavern and descended for a very long time. I was cold, but moving made it tolerable. We came to a level and then walked for miles down a tunnel.

There were torches every fifty feet or so, fed by a slight breeze that blew through.

After a long time, the temperature started to rise. Soon it had become uncomfortably warm. Then we came to an opening that might as well have been the entrance unto hell itself.

The stench emitted from that cavern was so powerful that I fell to the ground gagging. GT lifted me back up.

The garish cavern had a fissure down the center. Thirty or forty naked men and women labored hard with buckets and ropes, pluming the gash for black sludge that they then poured into a deep tub carved in the stone floor.

From another part of the cave, one naked man or woman after another dragged forward corpses that they dumped unceremoniously into the pit of muck. In the center of the man-made tub, the tar simmered, and every now and then a human crawled out and collapsed on the cave floor.

The smell of the room was foul. The light came from a hundred torches. The horror and power of the spectacle robbed me of my senses.

I must have lost consciousness, although I don't remember passing out. When I awoke, I was in a small rocky cavern that was rudely furnished with rugs made from fur, a table lashed together with hide, and a chair made in the same fashion. I was lying on a fur bed. GT and a brown primitive were hunkered down at my feet.

"Where are we?" I pleaded.

"The Wave," both men said together.

"What were you doing in that room?"

"Bringing back the dead tho that we can thurvive," the dusky man lisped. He had thick bones over almond-shaped eyes.

He was shorter than I, but his shoulders and thighs were immense. His hair was long and matted. His body stank. But his voice was surprisingly melodious — tenor and strong.

"What are you?"

"I am Veil Bonebreaker, firtht to climb the high mountain."

"And you are down here raising the dead?" I asked.

I wanted to keep talking. Anything to stave off insanity down there under the ground.

"Only a few," Veil said.

"There's a cemetery not far from here," GT added. "We need a few more bodies with knowledge on this world. And now that we know how to protect their minds, we are bringing them out for the last migration."

"But they were crawling out of that pit one after the other. You must have made thousands of people at that rate."

"Ith only our thecond revival," Veil said. "Arthurporter made it in time for our thelebration. In all, there are only three hundred and nineteen counth that are free. Nine hundred and fifty-theven for you."

"You were frozen?" I asked Veil.

"In the cold down here, until the Wave wathed over me."

"They plan to destroy you all," I said.

I had no power of conversation. I could say things, and I could ask, but not in any sequence or with any give-and-take. I was dead, that's how I felt. The words coming out of me were no more than the random last thoughts hemorrhaging out of a deceased brain.

"They have been developing a toxin. When they get it right, they're going to come after you with it."

"Thith mutht not happen," Veil said. "We mutht thurvive to the tranthithon."

"What's that?"

"Farsinger," GT said.

I knew immediately that it was the unique life-form that had cried out for a mate through the vacant ether.

"It's coming for you?" I asked.

"Yeth," Veil said.

"You are going to mate?"

"Unite," GT said. "Farsinger is one, and we are one and many. Together we will be seen across the sky."

"Migration," I said. "You're restless."

Both men smiled at me, their teeth glistening almost hungrily in the flickering light from the dying torch that lit my cave.

"We mutht thurvive," Veil said.

"We have to thurvive," Veil said for the fifth or sixth time.

I had fallen asleep again, and when I awoke, there was cooked rabbit on a rude stone dish sitting next to me. After I'd eaten, Veil came to me and spoke about the migration of the Wave.

"Long, long ago," he said, struggling with the language that he knew from GT and other dead Americans arisen from his sludge pit, "long before there were even fith in the othean, we heard Farthinger. Thee thang, and we rethponded, and then we began our rithe up from the deep, where we nethted and rethted, counting the many timeth we made the thircle.

"When we heard her, we rothe upward, knowing nothing but numberth and her call. Thee needth uth and cometh for uth. Thee is almotht here."

"How soon?" I asked the caveman.

"For uth," he said, "it ith an inthtant. For you, one thouthand five hundred and theventy-one dayth."

I tried to do the math in my head. I thought of the number, and instantly, 4.304 years came to mind.

"Am I infected with your tar?" I asked.

"Only thlightly," Veil said with his gentle lisp. "Enough to know thome of what we know and thome of how we think. We are no threat to you."

I believed this was true.

"Does every particle of the Wave know everything that you all know?"

"Half," Veil said. "We each know half the thame. The retht ith different for a billion counth, and then it thangeth again. We thare. We thame. We can come together and hold handth" — he smiled — "yeth, hold handth like loverth. All one and everything."

I remembered being a part of that school of mackerel. I had experienced the one and the many.

"What can I do?" I asked.

"Take uth with you back to thomeplathe thafe. Take uth with you and make uth thafe. In four yearth, all that we are will rithe up and become part of Farthinger. We will leave thith plathe and go out patht the blanket of pull."

"I will help you," I said.

On what I believe was my third day in the cave, GT announced that he was going to leave for a while.

"Where are you going?" I asked.

"To complete the penultimate part of my mission," he replied.

"What's that?"

"They are stalking us," he said. "One day they will find us. I must learn how to resist them."

I didn't know what he meant. I didn't want him to leave. But there was no room for questions or debate. One moment he was hunkered down next to me, smiling by torchlight, and the next he was walking away down a dark tunnel.

GT returned now and then, but never for very long. During these brief visits he would spend most of the time with one hand dipped into the stone tub that held the Wave.

29

I'm not certain how long I stayed in the cave of the Wave. There were no more revivals during that time. There were many strange things, however. Animals and birds came into the cave and communed with one another. There were about fifty men and women who had once lived but now were dead and resided permanently near the Tar of Life — the Wave. We talked together and laughed. When I was lonely, one of the women would sleep with me on the fur mat in the room where I had first met Veil.

Veil and I spent a lot of time together. We talked about the threats that humanity presented.

"We are not indethtructible," Veil said to me one day. "We are durable but not invulnerable. Your friend the plathtic thurgeon could dethtroy uth if you do not make uth thafe."

"How can I do that if you can't?" I asked.

"Becauth you are what our enemy ith,"

Veil replied. "We are only theeing without knowing."

I made a few friends while living down under the mountains. One such friend was Dick Ambler, a car salesman who had died seventeen years earlier. Unlike a great many of the humans that had been imbued with life, Dick was very lively, very much like a normal man. In his former life, he'd loved to tell funny stories, but since his revival, he didn't understand the meanings of the jokes in his mind. Sometimes he'd sit and tell me one of these jokes and I would try to explain why it was funny. He never really understood, but we became close anyway.

"How can the Wave be here and in Los Angeles at the same time?" I asked Dick one evening.

"We had been rising for a very long time under the city you call Los Angeles," he told me. "We sensed the music played by your DNA. But maybe three hundred years ago, we found a tunnel that led here. After discovering how dangerous men could be for us, the greater part of the Wave retreated to these caves, leaving only a few to reanimate the bodies."

★ ★ ★

I learned many things in the torchlight of that cave. At night, when I slept, I had visions of celestial beings communicating across the vastness of space. I could hear the vibrations of my own cells and read all species' histories through the coiled patterns of genes.

Once I put my hand into a bucket of black mud that Veil told me had all of the knowledge of the world inside it. At first it didn't feel like anything, but after a while, the heat began to build. Just when it became almost unbearable, I felt a shunt into my brain and all human sensations were gone.

I became an amorphous mass defined by ideas based on numbers rather than physical form or time. I could become a quartz melody or a woolly mammoth, but all of that was contained within a wider sense of being. Gravity and subatomic particles passed through me, massaged me. I encompassed even the shape of the universe.

I had feelings, but these, I saw, were inconsequential. I witnessed human slaughters and depravities, passions and virtues. All of this came to nothing. All except the loneliness of life. The Wave was one with itself and everything that it touched. It was Buddha and the Ten Thousand Things.

After only a few seconds with my hand in the bucket I collapsed.

On one of his sporadic visits, GT told me how much my father had loved me.

"When you were one and a half, you would come up on me on the couch," he said, "and climb up in my lap. You didn't talk very much, but you'd say, 'Sup, sup,' and then I'd say, 'Mongo time,' and you'd laugh and laugh. Nothing else made you laugh so much. You were my little boy, and I would have done anything for you."

"I found Bobby Bliss where you buried him," I said.

GT frowned. "Did your mother see him?"

"Do you care?"

"Very much," he said. "She loved that man and I destroyed him. It was wrong of me. But I was so angry."

As he spoke, the anger he had felt rose up in me again. The rage ran down into my fingertips, which then clenched into fists.

"I feel it," I said. "But Wheeler told me that the first XTs to rise from the grave didn't care about their relatives. Why do you care?"

"We squandered much of our substance to find the right touch," he said. "The first ones to rise, we pushed too hard, trying to make sure they did what we wanted them to. We learned after many costly mistakes that it didn't take a gallon but only an ounce to allow the man to be."

"So that's why some of the people revived by the Wave seem so distant?" I asked. "While others, like Dick Ambler, act more normal?"

"Yes."

"But why should it matter how much you use?" I asked. "Since the cells that make up the Wave are almost immortal, they aren't really squandered."

GT put his hands against his breast and said, "This part of the Wave cannot rise with Farsinger. Inside the body of man, we can only be man."

There was a deep sorrow in GT's voice. He was dreaming of the universe but was kept from it by the sacrifice he'd made to reach up into the atmosphere. He had become alienated from a life-form that he'd shared for millions of years. His feeling of loss permeated my mind. He was like a man walled into a crypt, fully alive and aware, with no hope of deliverance.

"But what about Veil?" I asked. "He was the first to rise. He seems to know what it means to be human."

"He has reincarnated himself many times," GT said. "Again and again until he got it right."

"But why?"

"He was the first," GT said, as if this was an explanation.

Together Dick Ambler and I helped Veil with grooming, to prepare him for the twenty-first century. There was water in the cave, so we washed him and cut his hair. We couldn't do much about his clothes. The wolves brought animals for me to eat, and Veil made clothing from their pelts.

I conversed with many of the risen dead in that cave. Most of them told stories about themselves in a removed manner, as if their previous lives had been fictions. They talked about loves they had felt and crimes they had committed.

One white man named Brad Ferguson told me that he had raped and murdered a dozen black farm workers and Chicano migrants he'd lured to his farm by promising them work.

"I killed them one after the other until one day a man named Pablo got away," the ghoul said, looking into my eyes. "A week later, he came back with two friends and slaughtered me."

"Do you regret what you did?" I asked, more than a little afraid of the man.

"I buried them in the basement of my house," Ferguson said. "I brought them all back, and they are among us now."

"Where do the people you raise go when they leave here?" I asked Veil soon after that conversation.

"They go out into the world looking for other depothith like ourth," he said. "We wonder if we are the only one that hath thurvived."

"There were other Waves?"

"Millionth of yearth ago," he said. "We moved out from the thame great depothit. Maybe the otherth ended. Maybe they are thtill moving up."

Veil made me a backpack from the hide of a deer. We filled it with the black tar, which was the Wave in its purest form. After the liquid was poured, it became a gelatinous whole — a giant ebony hard-boiled egg that quivered and gleamed.

"Is this the full knowledge?" I asked the primordial man.

"Yeth," he responded. "A billion yearth of evoluthon. A billion yearth of counting up to thith moment. One full athpect of all that we've been through and all that we've become."

I looked upon the jellylike mass with a sense of awe that I had never known.

I was tutored by the Wave during my sojourn in the cave. The few cells that connected my mind with the greater being had translated thousands of blueprints and histories, the evolution of life and the urge to grow. I often woke up exhausted from all the voices chattering in my head. Scuttling insects and great dinosaurs traveled in my mind, found their histories in me. I had come to see the sludge from the pit as God.

I would have died to save this being from Wheeler.

One day Veil and GT came to me. I hadn't seen the simulacrum of my father for quite some time and I was happy at first and greeted him with a smile.

"The wolves are dead," GT said.

"How?"

"Wheeler has made a bullet that enters the body and spreads a poison. They die as animal life dies. They are no more."

We mourned the wolves' passing. They had been the heart of the community we identified as home. Even though they'd had only the intelligence of beasts, they also had vibrated with the power and ambition and knowledge of the Wave.

The Wave was beyond the human experience of living and dying. Each aspect of the Wave — be it a cell, a group of cells, or a great construct, like the one that lived in my backpack — was physically connected to every other aspect of the greater being. This oneness made for a mind that was all-enveloping. For over a billion years, the Wave had no natural enemies, no reason to hate or fear or fight. It lived on elements and minerals developed from its natural interaction with its rocky environs. Its hypersensitive cells spoke to advanced beings far beyond our small part of the universe.

The sludge, the black tar that simmered and stank in the main cave, was far beyond human minds or human abilities.

"What is the smallest possible unit of the Wave that still has all of its knowledge?" I asked GT.

"About a pint," he said. "We're going to have you carry so much in case a part of us is destroyed along the way."

GT, Veil, and I went to the main cave. There GT dipped his hand into the tar. After a moment, the god began to tremble and then bubble. GT was also shaking. After a minute or two, he removed his hand.

"What just happened?" I asked GT.

There was a deep sadness in him.

"My human side," he said, "has taught the Wave to kill without mercy."

30

"I think I can hear them," I said.

All around, humans and cougars, coyotes and bears that had been resurrected by the Wave were readying themselves for battle. They set up barricades. Resurrected humans called upon their memories and armed themselves with clubs and stones.

I had seen the power of the Wave's zombies manifested. They each had the strength of half a dozen men and could not be mortally wounded by normal methods. But if Wheeler had prepared a toxin that could kill our wolves, all of my friends might soon die.

"I'll stay and fight," I told GT.

"No," Veil said. "You will be better out in the world. They may not find you ath eathily."

"But they suspect me already," I said. "That's why I had to run away."

"Let them tetht you," Veil said. "They will find nothing."

Veil and GT guided me to a passageway that I'd never noticed before. We had al-

226

ready entered when I heard an explosion and then a scream.

Katya — the granddaughter of Russian Jews, a woman who had made love to me almost every night for the past week — turned, revealing a deep gash in her chest. The edges of the wound began to dry and crack like baked mud. The cracks traveled Katya's whole body; her face was frozen in a paroxysm of pain. Her body became desiccated, then she collapsed to the stone floor and disintegrated into a pile of multicolored dust. Wisps of dry smoke rose from the remains of my long-dead lover.

Soldiers filled the room, carrying gaily colored red and yellow plastic rifles. They were shooting at the XTs without restraint. No one was asked if they wanted to surrender. The attack was meant to be a slaughter.

One of the soldiers pointed toward us. Veil grabbed my arm. "We mutht go," he said.

I wanted to turn away, but could not.

The soldiers took aim on our position. I stood in front so as to take the first shots and keep my father and my forefather alive.

But then a huge gout of tar shot up from

the Wave pit. It stuck to the ceiling and then sent out a dozen tentacles to pierce the bodies of the invaders.

Thousands of gallons of the tar rose up out of the pit and flowed down the way that the soldiers came.

"Run!" GT shouted.

I turned and ran with all my might.

I was able to keep up the pace for a half hour or so. Then I had to slow down. Veil slung me over his shoulder and continued running with no noticeable effect on his speed.

Down the long hall, we heard the sounds of humans screaming. Some were XTs and others not. At one point there was a powerful explosion. Maybe five seconds after that, I felt a pain go through my brain like an intense web of red-hot fibers. I yelled and hit the ground. It was death in my head, the death of the oldest, most intelligent species on the planet. The Wave had been blown out of its hole with Wheeler's toxin. We were dying by uncountable trillions because of men and their fear of being less.

I awoke in darkness. I felt around until I found GT and Veil. They were unconscious, too. My connection to the Wave was small, and I still felt the pain of its passing. It wouldn't have surprised me if Veil and GT had died from the trauma of losing their whole race.

After a while Veil came to.

"Do you thtill have the thack, Errolporter?" he asked me right off.

"Yes."

"Doeth it thtill live?"

We opened the fur pack together. The gleaming egg still shone and throbbed.

GT was up soon after Veil, and we continued our quick pace along the maze of underground tunnels. After many hours, we advanced toward a light. The sun was shining somewhere. I could smell the ocean. We hadn't spoken in all that time. The sorrow we felt was overwhelming. The oldest being in the world, maybe the oldest creature in the whole universe, had been slaughtered by a fearful beauty doctor.

I made up my mind to kill David Wheeler if ever I got the chance.

We left the cave on a mountainside that overlooked the calm Pacific. There was a beach a few hundred feet below but no people or boats or planes that I could see.

Veil took the backpack, and we scaled down the ridge. It was midday, and the air was cool. We made it to the beach in less than half an hour and almost immediately started marching north.

"Where are we going?" I asked my ancestors.

"To a city, Airy," GT said. "A place where we can hide our heritage and wait for Farsinger to come."

"How can that matter now? They murdered the Wave."

"No," Veil said. "We are alive in thith pouch. All we ever were and all we have known ith in there. You are in there, Errolporter. Everything ith."

A shot rang out, and Veil screamed in pain. There was a wound on his calf. He fell to the ground and ripped off the leg at the knee with a sickening sound of rending flesh and cracking bone. He was trying to pull out the wounded limb before the toxin traveled to the rest of his body.

At least six more shots rang out. I dove for the underbrush while GT dragged Veil behind me. Because of his superior strength, GT was able to climb higher into the shrubbery. After a few moments, we heard the fast and hard footsteps of soldiers. I could see them from my hiding place. In full fighting uniform, each one carried the bright yellow and red plastic rifles used to kill XTs.

Suddenly, a dozen feet above me, GT leaped up and threw two stones, one with each hand. These missiles struck two of the three soldier-boys in the head. I ran out with a stone in my hand and tackled the third soldier, whose attention had been diverted by the death of his friends. Once he was down, I began hitting him with the stone. He was dead long before I tired of striking him.

I had crushed his temples, but his face was still recognizable. It was Jerome, Krista's guard and lover. I vomited on his chest and then dragged myself away.

GT and I hid the bodies while Veil sat guard from higher up in the shrubbery. His leg had stopped bleeding but he was still feeling pain from the wound. We suspected that the toxin had made its way past the knee before his self-amputation.

We climbed up into the hills, using the cover of the coastal forest to hide from our pursuers. GT supported Veil by the shoulder while we made our way northward. We traveled through the night and into the next day. It was during our flight that I realized I had become stronger, hardier. I wasn't tired in the least.

Late the next morning, we came to the

outskirts of a mountain resort community.

We stole into an empty home in the hills. There was a car in the driveway and a key hanging from a bulletin board in the kitchen.

We also raided the closets for clean clothes that would make us less suspicious. I took a shower and shaved. So did GT. But Veil was in too much pain to do anything.

For hours we drove the back roads, hoping that Wheeler and his killers weren't waiting for us behind barricades.

31

Late that afternoon we were just south of San Francisco. By that time Veil's leg had disintegrated up to the hip socket.

"You will have to bury me," he said.

"We can't do that," I said.

"We must," GT said.

So we climbed back into the hills near San Mateo and dug a shallow grave for a man who had already been dead for ten thousand years. I remember throwing the dirt on his face. He didn't wince or grimace. He was passive to the last, saying nothing — at least not in words.

"He was at peace," GT told me as we drove our stolen car down along Lombard Street. "The life of the Wave and he are one. If the Wave continues, then he continues. His soul will rise in the sky, as will yours and mine when Farsinger comes."

We ditched the car and then registered at the Galaxy Motel on Lombard. GT had a pocketful of money that we used to pay for the room.

"Where'd you get the money, GT?" I

asked when we were finally alone. The room had two double beds and a small TV set upon a dark brown bureau.

"I took it from the bodies of soldiers I killed," he said with little, if any, emotion.

"Soldiers that attacked you?" I asked.

"No. They were looking for the cave, but they wouldn't have found it. They never saw me coming."

"Then why kill them?" A prickly feeling was running under my scalp.

"To learn how." GT turned his face to me. His eyes were galaxies; his skin, the void.

"Wh-why?"

"It is hard for us to commit violence," he said. "But we knew, we feared, that our survival might depend on the ability to murder. The mission was given to me to gain this ability, and then, if it was necessary, to share my experience with the Wave."

"You murdered for practice?"

GT nodded the assent of a cosmos.

"How many?" I asked.

He closed his eyes as if maybe he could blot out the number.

"Thirty-three," he said. "Stabbed, shot, strangled, dismembered. Some I killed slowly and others with great speed." Tears welled in his eyes.

"For no reason?"

"The reason is there," he said, gesturing at the leather backpack that held the Wave.

"Does that now contain your knowledge?" I asked.

GT gave me a wan smile.

"It has heard what I know, but it has not incorporated that knowledge physically," he said. "It knows my experience but is as yet unaffected by it."

I stared at my father, the murderer, and at the god, also a killer. I knew that it was only self-defense on the part of the Wave. It had to learn to kill in order to protect itself. I wanted to forgive, but could not. I wanted forgiveness for my lack of faith, but there was no one who could grant my wish.

"It can hear your thoughts?" I asked, not able to bear the silence.

GT nodded.

"Is that how you knew I'd be at Shelly's?"

"I didn't know you'd be there until you arrived."

"That makes no sense," I said. Inside I was battling numbness.

"Every night in the cave, did you have dreams?" GT asked.

"Yes."

"Dreams about confabulations between angels and celestial councils, gods and intellects, comprised of light?"

"Yes."

"Do you believe those dreams to be the product of your imagination?"

Gazing into his eyes I could still see vestiges of the cosmos. I shook my head and looked away.

"There is among the stars a unity," GT said. "A knowing and a language that is at once life and the expression of life. You, all of humanity, are the space before the first word in that dialogue. Your idiom is like the babble of an infant when its only notions are of hunger and of pain.

"I followed you to the orchard where Wheeler kept you prisoner. I didn't try to free you because your life is precious to me and to the Wave. I sensed you leaving with the soldier and the wife. I heard you climbing in the canyons and arrived at the same time. You are a part of me, Airy, a part of the Wave. I could follow you beyond the solar system, on to galaxies neither one of us could imagine."

"But why would you?" I asked.

GT grinned and reached out, touching my chest with his fingers, now the digits of a killer.

"Until we arrived at the detritus of genes toward the surface, we were unaware of life devouring itself. We had no concept of struggle or evil. Our discovery of life led us to try and understand. Veil was our first human. As we resuscitated others, we were amazed at their feelings and fear, and the violence in their hearts.

"Then other men captured our chosen. They imprisoned them, tortured them, and most of all, feared them.

"This body," GT said, touching his own chest with his other hand, "had already been washed by the Wave. It was set free to find one among humanity that would help us. You were that one."

"But why?" I asked again. "Why not someone smarter or more powerful? I can't help you."

"But you have," GT said. "You have loved us and seen through our eyes. You decided to help us even though we might have hurt you with our power."

"It doesn't make any sense. Why didn't you just kill Wheeler and Gregory and the people who plotted against you?"

"We didn't know how to kill except in self-defense. And even then, our violence had no plan, no logic."

"You had to learn if you were to deal with humans," I said.

"Yes."

We sat there staring at each other. I had never been closer to my father. He had never been so far from me.

"That was my mission," he said after a while.

"What was?"

"To find you and learn the ways of humans. To learn to fight them once they decided we should die."

"Why let them find you in the first place?" I asked.

"Veil didn't have the wherewithal to fight us. His kind would fear us, but they couldn't hurt the Wave. It wasn't until after we had resuscitated hundreds that we realized humans might be a threat."

"It's just that they're afraid you'll take over the earth," I said, feeling that I had to defend our stupidity.

"But Wheeler must know that we multiply very slowly. If we grew one percent in a million years, that would be amazing. And often our numbers recede. The Wave is everlasting. Population is not our priority. He knew at least some of this from his studies. You told us as much."

"Maybe he thought there were many more of you, enough to take over all the people of the world."

"He was afraid that we wanted to be

human? That would be like you wanting to crawl into a snail shell, like a whale wanting to inhabit a pond."

"Humans believe they're the most important creatures in the universe," I said. "It's hard for us to think that you wouldn't want what we have."

"Or maybe they know that the Wave is superior to man. Maybe we present an end to the dream of humankind as the rulers of all they see."

"But they had to wonder why you would take human form in the first place," I said. "I mean, was it only a posture of defense?"

"Not only; we also wanted to experience the human equation," GT said. "To share with you what we knew of life. We were coming to the surface anyway. At first we wanted to show you how far you might go. We see now that it was a great mistake."

"Wheeler and his people thought you wanted to take over the world."

"The Wave is not vermin, Airy. That province is held solely by man."

There was nothing about XTs or the slaughter in the caves on the news. Bush was still threatening war in Iraq. The North Koreans were saying that they had the bomb. Millions were dying of AIDS in Africa, and Norah Jones had won five Grammys.

I woke up once in the middle of the night. GT was hunkered down next to the backpack. He had taken the metal scoop from the ice machine in the parking lot. With this he ladled out a large portion of the Wave. This he was pouring into his mouth.

"What are you doing?" I asked him.

The sounds he made were like the strangulation of a whole herd of bison. He waved me away and then went back to his feast. His gesture brought on a great exhaustion in me. I staggered back to the bed and collapsed.

GT was gone when I woke up. He had left me a note before going this time.

Airy,

I'm going now because I can only bring you trouble. They'll be looking for me a little harder than you. So take our Soul and put it somewhere Wheeler and his soldiers will never find it. Then run, son. Run deep into the world and keep your head down. Remember, God is in you now. You are forever and the light.

Your father

I wandered the environs of San Francisco for the next few days. There was no reason to believe that Wheeler and his band of murderers knew I was there. I looked everywhere for a place to secret the greatest treasure in the world. I went from Coit Tower to the San Francisco Zoo to Fisherman's Wharf.

Finally, I came upon the statue of a lion in Golden Gate Park. It was six feet high and over nine feet long, standing upon a great marble dais. It was a hollow bronze icon that had been there for over a hundred years. I waited until late at night and then sneaked up on the regal metal beast. There were holes where the nose was. I opened my backpack near the snout, and the black tar began to tremble. Suddenly it gushed forth and into the great sculpture. For thirty seconds, I watched God slither into hiding, and when he was gone, I feel down on my knees, exhausted from what seemed like a lifetime of hard labor.

For nearly a year after that, I lived in and around the Mission District, washing dishes when I had to, crashing at various homeless shelters when I couldn't raise the money for a five-dollar room. My hair got long, and for the first time in my life, I grew a beard. I lost a lot of weight and took up the habit of drinking wine after the sun went down.

I wasn't a real wino, like some of the people down there. I'd take a few slugs to be sociable and to cut the edge on all that I'd lost. Every now and then I thought about Nella Bombury. Once I even called her, but her number had been disconnected.

The saving grace of my life was the dreamtime that the Wave brought me. The XTs in me sang of all their history. A thousand beings arisen from the dead chanted to me every night and day, telling me their stories. Housewives and cave bears, scientists and jellyfish, all together, alive inside me. They moved together with my own consciousness. I was the many and the one.

Every now and then, some tough in the street would pick a fight with me. Sometimes it was to steal what little money I had, other times just because he didn't like the way I looked. But as the days passed, the Wave made me stronger. I could hold my own against most enemies, and even if I lost against a gang, I healed quickly.

The days went by without much to mark them. I got thinner and stronger and often could be found wandering down along the wharves, talking to one of the souls that inhabited my mind.

I never went near the bronze lion in the park. I never went to the park at all, just in case one of Wheeler's agents was on my trail.

As the days passed, I became lighter in my heart. My wife's infidelity and my father's crimes lost meaning. I worried about my sister at times, but I knew going to her would only get me arrested.

The newspapers, which I read almost every day, had nothing to say about XTs or mass exterminations of that ancient species. GT never appeared in the news; nor did any other strange being with extraordinary powers.

Twelve months from the day that I had poured the Wave into that bronze lion, I had a waking dream.

Liliane Modesto, a young woman who had died of AIDS in 1996, came to me. She wore a sheer slip and no shoes or makeup. It was the way she thought of herself. I suppose she looked about twenty.

"You can go back to your life whenever you want," she said to me.

I was sitting on a stone bench in front of the opera house in San Francisco, but she and I were perched on a red rock at Joshua Tree National Park on a bright day when no one else was there.

"You are free now," Liliane said.

"But what about the Wave?" I reasoned. "What if they capture me and find out where it is hidden?"

"You don't remember," she said, and I realized it was true. Part of my memory had been blocked, temporarily, as it turned out. I knew nothing of the Wave's whereabouts. I couldn't betray my God.

Liliane came over and sat on my lap. She kissed me, and I was ashamed because my clothes were filthy and I hadn't bathed in over a week.

"You're beautiful to me," she said. "You are our hero. The greatest hero in the longest history on earth. You have even saved the Farsinger, who surely would have died of loneliness if we were not here awaiting her."

I don't know what the people around me thought. Some bearded black bum pretending to be holding a woman, sticking out his tongue in a show of pitiful passion.

32

I went to work for a fishermen's collective just south of San Francisco. My job was to help unload boats every morning from four-thirty to noon. Within five weeks, I had enough money for a suit of used clothes and a bus ticket to L.A. The Wave dreams subsided, and I could pay attention to my surroundings. I kept my long hair and beard, figuring that Wheeler's agents might not notice me if I looked older and thin.

I bought a short-handled shovel and a bag to hold it in and then, the night before I was to leave, I took a BART train over to Berkeley. Under a light of the crescent moon, I climbed up into the semi-wilderness of Pioneer Park. My night vision had improved under the influence of the Wave, so it was easy to find my way to a place that was mostly isolated. There I climbed deep into the bushes and began digging my hole.

When the pit was maybe three feet deep, I took out my journal, which I had wrapped in an oilcloth. It was now a thousand pages long, ragged and uneven, filled with incomprehensible space languages that I now spoke with some fluidity. I refilled the hole, then covered it with leaves and branches, even though it was unlikely that anyone would ever come across it.

In the morning I headed to the Greyhound station and made the daylong journey back home.

I got to Nella's apartment building at around eleven on a Thursday evening. I felt nervous there, knocking on the door. Her phone had been disconnected. She had probably moved, too.

A big man who wore only jeans answered. He was black and heavily muscled, with dreadlocks and a clean-shaven young face.

"Yes?" he said as a challenge.

"Nella," I replied.

"What you want wit' her?" he asked me.

"Nella," I said a bit louder.

"Who?" she said from somewhere beyond the young African godling.

"It's me, Nella. It's Errol."

"What?"

Nella ran to the door, pushing aside her new man. She looked at me with wide bright eyes and then folded me into her arms.

"You're so skinny," she said. "And what's all this hair? Where have you been, baby?"

"Who is dis man?" Nella's new man friend asked.

"Not now, Roger," she answered. "Not now. This is an old friend who I t'ought was dead."

"Well, you need to tell him that it's too late to be droppin' by people's houses," Roger said.

"When you get your own house, you can tell your guests whatever you want," she snapped. "But until then, move out of my way so I can show this man a seat."

Roger wanted to hurt me, I could see that in his face. But I wasn't worried. There were tears in my eyes as I looked upon Nella. She meant as much to me as did GT or even the Wave. That moment might have well been my first true experience of adult human love.

"Where have you been, Errol?" Nella asked after seating me at the kitchen table. "Can I get you some water? You need something to eat."

"Have you heard from my sister?" I asked.

"She's fine, and so is the baby. She

named her Aria after she came out of the hospital, and she was so sick, too."

"But she's better now?"

"She's an angel."

"That's good."

"Now, where have you been?" Nella asked me.

I didn't know where to start, so I just looked at her.

When the front door broke open, I knew instantly what was happening.

Nella screamed. Roger came running out of the bedroom, where he had retreated. Six or seven men in dark suits, carrying guns, ran in on us. I was thrown to the floor, and so were Roger and Nella.

They put handcuffs on me and covered my head with a bag while Nella cursed at them.

I didn't know what they were doing with me, but it didn't matter. I was safe from their machinations, their plans to murder a superior being. All of the kicks and punches were reminders that I had defeated mankind and saved the Black God of Earth.

I was thrown into a dark, damp cell. They took the bag off my head, but my hands remained chained behind my back.

At one point three men came in and took blood samples from my arm. I didn't fight them. I didn't worry about the darkness or the cold. Many a night in San Francisco, I had slept on the street when the fog brought a chill in that went right through me. My hands hurt only until they went numb. And the Wave returned to me. It whispered rousing tales of dung beetles and crocodiles. I flowed through a dozen life-forms before the door to my cell opened again. I immediately recognized the silhouette in the hall.

"Dr. Wheeler," I said.

"Hello, Errol."

Two soldiers came and in and pulled me to my feet. They took off my chains. I squinted past them at the green-eyed mass murderer.

"How's your wife?" I asked him.

"Thank you for asking," he said pleasantly. "She was killed in an automobile accident two months after you escaped."

The next day found us in the secret bunker where I had first seen the atrocities that Wheeler had committed. We were sitting in a comfortable room with wooden chairs and a long Formica-topped table. Wheeler served me coffee and sweet buns.

He was smiling in a most self-assured manner.

"Where have you been?" he asked me.

"San Francisco."

"What were you doing there?"

"Hiding from you."

"What did I ever do to make you fear me, Errol?" Wheeler seemed almost pained. "You were a guest in my house."

"Krista told me that Dr. Gregory wanted to classify me XT. I decided to run."

I could see that David Wheeler was surprised by his wife's betrayal. He was more hurt by that disloyalty, it seemed, than he was by her death.

"What did you do in San Francisco?"

"Lived in the streets, drank wine, got into fights."

"Where's GT?"

"He left me long ago. Before I even met you."

Wheeler stared at me. He sensed that I was more of an opponent than I had been sixteen months earlier.

"The XTs are all dead," he said.

"Then how could you be looking for GT?"

"The deaths are absolute. The victims are disintegrated, turned into dust. The dead were never identified."

"You killed them all?"

"Almost," Wheeler said with a half-smile. "After further testing, Gregory found out that the infection is not communicable. We destroyed the pit that held the contagion, but we left a few of the ghouls alive to study. Come with me."

He led me to an elevator that went down to the prisoner level of XT-1. Standing there, I remembered my vow to kill him. But he had said that some of the XTs were still alive. If I attacked him, his soldiers would surely slaughter me. In order to help my father's race, I held back.

The doors opened in the wide hall of cells that I had witnessed so long ago. On my right was the room where the man had sat in the cage filled with carbon monoxide. All of the cells we passed were empty. Some of them contained piles of multicolored dust, marking the passing of demigods.

After a long walk, we came to a door that led to a smaller hall. Here there were five glass-walled cells. Four of these were occupied by prisoners — two men and two women.

One of the men was GT.

He waved at me and mouthed *Airy.*

"Here is the last of the infestation," Wheeler proclaimed. "Broken down and destroyed, unable to leave the corpses they inhabit. Our work here has saved the world."

"Why did you ask about my father if you knew he was alive?"

"To see what you would say."

It was then that I recommitted myself to Wheeler's death. I was about to jump on him, when I was grabbed by four strong men who rushed in behind me. They chained me hand and foot and then threw me into the empty glass cage.

I was ranting, screaming, cursing at Wheeler.

"You're the criminal!" I shouted. "You're the one who needs to die!"

"I'm not a criminal," he said. "I didn't commit genocide. I merely contained a pathogen. You can see that I've left some of the specimens alive, here in my own private zoo."

He grinned, showing all of his teeth. I realized that somehow along the way, the plastic surgeon had gone mad.

33

"Don't worry, Airy," a voice in my head said. "He believes that we are defeated, and so we are victorious."

The other three inmates — an Asian man who wore a name tag that said MON-GOOSE, and two young women named Penelope and Renata — were silent.

By that time I was uncertain about what had really happened with me. There was something about GT that made me nervous and afraid, but I couldn't remember what. And then there was the Wave. It was somewhere . . . San Francisco, I thought.

"He will test you, son," GT whispered in my mind. "He will push you hard. But rejoice. He can never win, and you, Errol, can never lose."

GT's meaning came clear within the next few minutes. Wheeler returned to the cell block with two men wearing nylon protective suits and carrying a metal canister connected to a corrugated plastic hose. They attached the hose's nozzle to a conduit on my cell. When one of them turned a knob, I could hear the hissing of gas, and I detected a slight sweet odor.

My heart started beating fast and faster; my head felt as if it were under heavy pressure.

I awoke on the cot in my cell. Wheeler was standing outside, looking down on me.

"You died, Mr. Porter."

"Then why the fuck am I still lookin' at your ugly face?"

"Well" — he smiled — "almost died. The gas we gave you has no effect on these other monsters. So I guess you're still human. How are you feeling?"

"Like shit."

"Pull yourself together. You have a guest."

The other glass cells were empty.

"Where are the others?" I asked Wheeler.

"We make the exhibits go into their dens most of the time. To be out here is a privilege that they rarely enjoy. Gregory wanted to see how they reacted to you. It was, once again, a disappointment."

"Who's my guest?"

Wheeler smiled and left the cell block.

While I was unconscious, they had dressed me in pale blue cotton hospital pants and a white T-shirt. Looking in the small mirror that hung on the back wall of the cell, I found that my beard and mustache were gone and that my hair had been cut close to the scalp. My face seemed at once younger and older. I was thinking about that when I caught the reflection of Nella walking into the room.

"Baby!" she yelled.

She ran up to the glass and pressed her body against it.

She was wearing a conservative green dress and white pumps.

"Nella." I was up against the glass, too. "Are you with that guy now?"

"Roger was only stayin' awhile," she said.

I thought it was funny that, after all we had gone through, our first words were so petty. But it seemed right that we were talking about jealousies and insecurities in spite of our suffering.

"How did you find me?" I asked.

"They arrested me when they got you," she said. "They brought me here to betray you, Errol. They want me to find out the secret of your father. I told them I would, but it was only so I could get in here to tell you that I love you. I loved you ever since you first came to work at Mud Brothers. You know that, don't you? I used to stand there next to you, hoping you would ask me out. I always wanted you. I broke up with my old boyfriend the day after our first date. I never told you, because I thought it would scare you off. And then, when you disappeared, I thought you would never know." She was still up against the glass, her breasts pressed flat under her green dress.

"They arrested me, honey," I said. "They took me. I tried to call, but your phone was disconnected. I thought you had gone away."

Her tears rolled down the glass barrier.

"You fool," she said. "I needed a cell phone, and I didn't want two bills. You shouldn't have come back."

"Oh yes, I should have, too," I said.

I could see my brown face in the glass, superimposed on Nella's dark grief. My heart swelled. Three men came. They grabbed Nella and pulled her from the glass wall. With all of her weight, she tried to defy them, but they were the superior force.

Her screaming my name was both pain and hope for me.

Nella knew nothing of what I had been through, but she was still brave and unflinching, risking her own freedom just to tell me that I was her man.

Wheeler came in a few minutes later.

"You must have some kind of power over women, Errol," he said. "My wife, this girl. What do they see in you?"

"An innocent man being tortured by a fiend," I said.

He laughed. I had the feeling that he was taking in his own reflection, as I had done when looking at Nella. Maybe all we could see was ourselves, I thought. Maybe that was why the Wave had to flee the planet.

Flee the planet. The words seemed to be right, but I no longer knew what they meant.

"Where did you go, Errol?"

"I already told you."

"You didn't show up in the Bay Area until almost four months after you escaped my house."

I was silent then. The connections were too close to the cave where I sojourned with Veil. And GT? Where was he during that time?

"Where were you before then?" he asked.

"I moved up the coast," I said. "Hitchhiking and camping."

"Tell me the places where you stayed."

"Santa Barbara." Sweat was running

down my back. "On the beach. I begged in the mall downtown for money to eat with."

"Who did you hang out with?"

"I didn't have any friends."

"I don't believe you, Errol."

"All you have to do is send your spies up there," I said. "They'll prove it."

"Yes," the madman replied. "But you better not be lying. Nella is going to be staying here with us — as a kind of a material witness. She's going to be staying until we get the truth out of you."

"You can't hold her," I said.

"I can do a lot more than hold her, Errol. I can do a lot more than that."

The wall at the back of my cell rose up, revealing a tiny chamber with a single cot, a toilet, and a sink. Wheeler told me to go in, and I obeyed, quailing in my heart over Nella and my helplessness.

I didn't know where the Wave was hidden, but I was pretty sure it was in San Francisco. That knowledge alone was too dangerous to hold.

I couldn't let them hurt Nella.

I couldn't let them destroy the oldest being in the world.

When the wall came down, I screamed in the dim light of my small cell. Then I sat down on the bunk and brought my head to my knees.

For over an hour, my heart raced and my mind tried to find some way out of my troubles. Once Wheeler found that there was no one who'd seen me in Santa Barbara, he'd come down on Nella or make me detail my days in the cave. I didn't think I could come up with a believable lie. And he could use drugs to force the truth from me.

I rolled up into a ball on the floor, hating myself for being so helpless. Why had I come back to Los Angeles? I was a fool. A fool.

I fell asleep for only a moment, and the solution came to me: I'd kill myself. That was the only way.

My first thought was to hang myself, but there were no sheets or blankets on the mattress. My cotton pants might have made a good rope, but I couldn't find anything to hang them from. There wasn't even enough room for me to run headfirst into the wall. Wheeler had put me in a suicide-proof room.

I sat on the floor, looking at the dull gray wall under the minimal lighting. I must have been sitting there for hours before I came up with the answer.

There was no plug for the shallow zinc sink, but my T-shirt stuffed down the drain did the trick. I filled the basin with warm water and washed my face. Then I plunged my head down and took a deep liquid breath, thinking of the mackerel I had been in a previous life held over in my DNA.

I grasped the sink and stood as long as I could, refusing to exhale the water from my lungs. At first it was almost unbearable, but then everything became pleasant and warm. The light faded, and I felt my feet slipping to the side. Still I held on, and then everything seemed to stop.

34

There was a buff desert that went on forever under a red sun. It was midday. It was always midday. There was only the desert and the heat seething upward. There was no past or future. There was no me. But after many eons of desert and sun, something happened: small bumps appeared along the surface of the land. The bumps grew into mounds that cracked open, and green shoots lanced upward. The bulging heads of the plants flowered as they rose toward the sun, and I came into being realizing that life struggled under the ground. The flowers were yellow and red, and they had voices, loud and shrill voices. A billion billion tiny flower-alarms went off. They were deafening, so I found my hands. I covered my ears. I squatted down and pressed my knees against my hands against my head. But the shrill sound of the yellow and red flowers went on and on. It was a wall of sound, a mountain of sound. I could see it, feel its weight on me. And then he came out of it — GT. Naked again, as he was when I found him. But he wasn't smiling anymore.

"Why are you doing this?" he asked me.

"What?"

"Killing yourself. Taking your life away."

"I can't betray Nella or the Wave," I said.

"You couldn't betray us even if you wanted to. But for the girl, if you live, tell them to come to me."

GT moved away from me, and as he did, the sound subsided. The flowers withered and died as the sun moved toward an infinite desert horizon. It became colder and darker until I was chilled down to the bone, looking into a world so black that I might as well have been blind.

I was a corpse floating in a lifeless ocean. There was no sun. No light of any kind. Just the frigid embrace of the ocean, which was also Death. There was no more Errol. Just the memory of him. That memory held few details, no aspirations, and it was unraveling until soon there would be only the cold.

And then there was light.

It was a cold light far above my eyes. It was as if I had no body, as if my eyes saw only at a distance. I had died and returned into a world where there was no grace or comfort or even pain.

For a long time I wondered if Death was a great mausoleum where the dead were put into long drawers of cold, pure light. This idea made the most sense to me.

But as I watched the light, I began to see irregularities. Fibers and crystal, filaments and pulse.

It was a lightbulb, a mechanical thing hovering above the gurney I was laid out on, in the infirmary of Dr. Wheeler's XT-1 command center.

"How are you, Errol?" Wheeler asked.

"I thought I was dead," I uttered. My voice was hoarse and cracked. It hurt my lungs to speak.

"You said that you were in Santa Barbara, but you weren't, were you?"

"No," I said, obeying the dictum of a dream.

"Where were you?"

"In a cave where the XT had fully surfaced. A place far in the coastal mountains."

Wheeler's smile was maniacal. "And what was your mission?"

"To preserve part of the life-form."

"So that it could somehow take control in San Francisco?"

"No. It was only trying to survive, to get away from you."

"What else?"

"I don't know all of it," I said honestly. "The Wave had concentrated all of its knowledge into that one sample of itself. Like I said, it wanted only to survive."

"And where is it?"

"GT knows," I said.

My body was returning to life. I could feel pinpricks of pain up and down my arms and legs. The ache filled me with a kind of masochistic joy.

"Kill him now," a voice said.

I couldn't see him, but I knew it was Dr. Gregory, Wheeler's partner in genocide.

"No," David Wheeler said. "We need him to make GT give us what we need."

I struck a deal with the army's scientists. I would enter GT's cell and get him to tell me what they needed. In return, I would be forgiven my treason and allowed to go off with Nella. I accepted their offer even though I had begun to believe that GT had never spoken to me, that it was all just a dream.

GT's glass cell was empty when they marched me in. They opened his cubicle, locked me inside, and then the back wall rose up, revealing the black youth who claimed to be my father.

"Airy," he said with a smile.

He walked up and put his arms around

me. I returned his loving embrace with a Judas hug.

"Why did they bring you here?" he asked.

"Said that they wanted to see how we interacted," I said. "I think that Gregory thinks I'm one of you."

"You are of me," GT said. "You're my son."

"What's going on, Dad?" I asked. "Why don't they kill you all?"

The corners of GT's eyes got tight, just as my father's had when he suspected that I was lying.

"Don't you remember, boy?"

"Help me," I said. "If I don't find out, they'll kill Nella. If you love me, you'll tell them. I don't want her to die."

Even now, looking back on that moment, I don't know what I felt. Was I trying to betray GT or doing what I thought was right? I had seen and dreamed so much that I no longer knew what was real and what was not. All I could do was move forward and hope that in doing so, things would work out fine.

"You want me to betray the Wave?" he asked.

"You've already lived a long life," I said. "Please, let us live."

265

35

We were both manacled hand and foot. GT's restraints were three times thicker than mine. I wondered how he managed to walk through the woods with all of that weight on him. As it was, he moved slowly, dragging along like a sloth.

There were three guards armed with the specially built plastic guns used to kill XTs. GT had led us to a place in the woods about three miles from the cave I'd lived in for three months.

For all I knew, he was leading Wheeler to the last vestige of the Wave. But there was nothing I could do about it. All I knew was that I couldn't let Nella die and that I was powerless between man and monster (though I didn't know then which was which).

"Where are we?" Wheeler asked GT.

"In the woods," he said. "In the woods."

"Don't play with me, thing. We have your son. I'll kill him right here if you don't show us the contagion."

GT looked at the mad plastic surgeon

and then at the soldiers who stood at his side.

We were in a clearing where a stream ran through and two oak trees stood. The sun was high, and there was a mild breeze. I felt a yearning to be alone in that spot, to be free of my manacles and the madman, of buried secrets and guilt.

"I am what you are looking for," GT said. "I am the memory of a thousand thousand thousand years."

He stood up straight, seemingly unhindered by the weight of his irons. The soldiers instinctively moved to block GT from Wheeler, raising their plastic weapons. They had no idea that every move they made had been planned for.

"Stand down," one of the soldiers commanded.

GT moved faster than I would have believed possible, even for one of his kind. He yanked his arms and legs apart, shattering the chains that held his manacles. Then he struck three times, killing each soldier before a shot could be fired.

Wheeler took a step backward and fell, then rose. GT was on him in an instant. He grabbed the doctor by his arm. GT's fingers clutched at Wheeler's chest. Our tormentor's scream made me move toward them. I wanted to end his pain, to save him from the torture that my father was inflicting. But as I approached, there was a shot. GT stopped, and his body went rigid. Cracks appeared in his back and legs, and then he turned to dust.

Wheeler stood there gasping for breath. There was a yellow and red plastic pistol in his left hand.

Wheeler used a cell phone to call for help. I was returned to my prison. The other XTs had been destroyed while we were out in the woods. I was alone in the glass prison, the only survivor of Wheeler's terrible war. I don't know how long I was held there. I got meals twice a day, but there was no other way to mark the passage of time. I never saw the guard who brought my food, because I had to go behind the wall before he'd leave the tray in the glass cell.

Afterward I found that I'd been imprisoned for fourteen months.

In all that time, I saw no one, spoke to no one. It was during that period that I lost hope and faith. How could all that I remembered be true? The only proof was my prison cell. But maybe I was just crazy and this was the mental institution that housed me.

I often dreamed about Wheeler. He'd come in and taunt me, telling me that I would never be free because of my relationship with his wife. He'd brag about killing my father and Nella and even Dr. Gregory.

I had those dreams every night. After a while I began to believe that they weren't dreams at all, that Wheeler really met with me, but I repressed those meetings into fantasies that I experienced again as dreams. I thought that he was my psychiatrist and that the dreams were stories I made up to hide from the reason I was institutionalized. I spent my days trying to decipher Wheeler's intentions. Maybe I had killed Nella, or maybe I felt guilty for the death of my father. I had resurrected him with the complex fantasy of a life-form deep in the earth, in the earth where my father had been buried.

My hair had grown long again (or maybe for the first time). I ate less every day. I thought about killing myself. I even filled the basin with water once. But the memory of those screaming flowers dampened my will.

After a very long time, Wheeler came to visit me. Green-eyed and tall, he no longer seemed insane.

"Am I cured?" I asked him.

"You're free," he replied.

"I'm sane?"

Wheeler smiled. "Freedom and sanity have never really gone hand in hand, my boy."

"Where is Nella?" I asked Wheeler.

"Living her life somewhere, I suppose."

"Where are the others?" I asked.

Wheeler seemed sad, as if he regretted the senselessness that had been his life for so long.

"You are all that's left," he said.

"And what now?" I asked.

"You're free," the doctor said again.

He led me down a long empty hallway that was minimally lit. There were no other inmates, soldiers, scientists, or guards. The whole complex seemed deserted.

"Is Dr. Gregory still around?" I asked Wheeler.

"He died."

"Died of what?"

"Natural causes, they say. He had been given a promotion. He moved to the Bay Area, and then, two days after being in office, he had a massive coronary. It's funny. He never had heart problems before.

"They called me to take his place. I told them they'd have to let you go if I agreed."

We had come to a door labeled PROPERTY.

"Why?" I asked. "I was part of the enemy. At the very least, I was a traitor."

"A boy's father defies death and returns home, and his son loves him. That's not treason."

Wheeler opened the door. There were hundreds of boxes with various XT codes written across their sides. Property of the dead. I remembered then the place where we had buried Veil. It was the first time I'd had that image in my mind since I had experienced the partial amnesia that kept the bronze lion hiding place from my mind.

But now, all of a sudden, I remembered everything.

Wheeler handed me a small cardboard box containing the few belongings I'd left behind.

"There's a little money in your wallet," Wheeler said. "And Nella Bombury's cell phone number."

"Why are you letting me go?"

"Because it's over, Errol. Your part in this is over. The entity is destroyed. We're still studying the aftereffects. And we're scouring the planet to look for other deposits. But we think that this was the only one."

"I slept with your wife."

"I abandoned her long before she ever strayed. And you weren't the only one."

"I killed Jerome," I said. "I beat in his skull with a rock when he was shooting at Veil and GT."

"We lost dozens of soldiers when the battle came. Every one of them has a fiction built around his demise. I think that Jerome Mathers died in a rock-climbing accident."

Wheeler's green eyes gazed upon me until I turned away. At first I walked, but then I ran from that building. I was the sole survivor of a war that had nearly slaughtered an entire race.

36

Nella took me back. She had been living with Roger again, but between the time I called her and the time I got there, he had been moved out. I told her it was okay that she'd had another man.

"That means you have another girl-friend," she said. "And where is she?"

"It was more than one, honey," I said. "But they're all dead now."

"What have they done, baby?" she asked.

"They killed God because he smiled on them."

GT proved to be part of my life even after he was destroyed by Wheeler. He'd been caught because he came to see my sister after finding out that her daughter was so sick. He went by the house and sprinkled sand on her. After a few hours, all of Aria's bodily functions normalized, and she became the perfect child.

When I saw Aria, I knew that she was like me, lightly dredged in the Wave, mildly aware of the Rapture that once thrived beneath our feet.

My mother had died while I was gone. She'd become despondent. She had buried Bobby Bliss next to my father's grave, in the plot that had been meant for her. Then she began to lose her memory. Angelique and Lon took her in until one day she tried to walk Aria on a leash. Then they put her in the same nursing home where my father's mother ended her days.

I was sorry I never got the chance to talk to her again.

Nella and I had twins. They have black skin and curly golden hair. One a boy named Arthur Bontemps Porter IV, and the other a girl named Luna, after the mistress who calls in the waves.

Nella and I started our own pottery production line, and life became steadier than it had ever been. Shelly went back to New York and married Thomas. Nella and I attended the wedding on Long Island.

More than two years after I got back into my life, I started having dreams again. I would be in the cave with Veil and Dick Ambler. They were telling me things about the Farsinger and the moment of alignment.

"You know that I'll always be a part of you," my father told me in a dream.

"It's just so crazy, Dad," I said.

"Alignment is in two weeks," he said. "You should be there."

"But what if Wheeler is still following me? I mean, he might figure out what's going on and kill the last Wave."

"Go."

That's how I ended up in front of the bronze lion. It was a clear afternoon, and San Francisco was buzzing with the unexplained appearance of the Northern Lights in its daytime sky. The waves of light, like multicolored curtains, didn't surprise me; they spoke. They talked about a long journey from a place so small that I couldn't imagine it and about a place she had come from that was nothing like anything she'd ever witnessed except the Wave. It was a song that made me tremble. Through the magic of Farsinger, I could see past the edge of the universe.

That afternoon the lights got stronger. Hundreds of people were pointing upward, taking photographs. I sat on a park bench across from the big bronze lion, feeling that if I died that very instant, my life would be remembered beyond the lifetime of most stars.

"Beautiful, isn't it?" David Wheeler said.

I hadn't heard him come up or felt him take a seat at my side.

"I expected you, David."

"Call me Papa, Airy," he said in a tone that I could not mistake.

"You took over his body before he could shoot you," I said.

He smiled in response.

"But I thought that once the Wave had resurrected you, you couldn't do that."

"You remember seeing me eat from the Wave?" he asked in answer.

I remembered seeing him pour the black tar into his mouth in our motel room.

"I carried it inside me," he said. "And when I was taken to our cell, it migrated from my body and hid until they took us to the woods that day. When I grabbed him, the tar went into him through my fingers, and so even as I died, I was also reborn."

"Is that why you learned how to murder?" I asked. "To prepare yourself to kill those soldiers?"

"Partly," Wheeler said with my father's inflections. "I also taught the Wave in the cave to kill with the logic of humans."

"And Wheeler?" I asked. "Is he dead, too?"

"No. He's still around."

"Do you control him?"

"Only inasmuch as I relieve the pressure he feels. He was a tortured madman, and now he feels good most of the time, reflective. I think he's a little suspicious of why he let you go. But after a dozen tests, he hasn't been able to find any XT activity in his system."

"And so you follow him around? Hiding in his skin?"

"I follow you and Angelique and Aria. I'm in contact with those whom Wheeler's men never found. We're looking for others like us in the earth. And we're trying to have a good influence on the world."

"But what about —"

"Sshh," Wheeler/Dad said.

He pointed at the sky above the bronze lion. I felt a thrill go through me. It was like an electric shock. The curtain of light seemed to open into blackness right above the statue. The lion's head glowed red. People around began shouting and running. The shock to my system was so great that I fell to the concrete and shook uncontrollably. Wheeler/Dad was standing over me, laughing. The lion's head exploded, and the Wave gushed up into the hole presented by Farsinger's light.

I could feel and see every cell as they rose and expanded to incredible sizes. My mind was sucked up into the vast being that was so large, only the smallest portion of her celestial body could be contained in our solar system. Trillions of what Wheeler called XTs flew up at incredible speeds, becoming the size of elephants, whales, small hills, and later on, even planets. My head was as large as the moon out past the farthest planet. The pulsating, spinning joy of the Farsinger tore me apart and then re-assembled me. GT was there, and Veil, and so was I.

The Wave absorbed the radiant being of this alien life-form, and together they transformed into something completely different. The XTs changed their structures, and Farsinger altered her song. They formed into a long chain of interconnected notes that moved away with greater speed than either had known was possible. Their departure felt like a great suction through my mind, my soul. I screamed, and so did Wheeler.

When I awoke, we were lying in hospital beds side by side.

"What were you doing there, Errol?" was his first question, and I knew that GT was letting him be in charge.

"I don't know, David. I just had an urge to come to Frisco. I wanted to see those lights."

"Why were you in the park?"

"I saw you go there," I lied. "I followed you, wondering if the light had something to do with the XTs."

I was discharged in a few days. Nella had come up with Luna and Artie. They took me back home, and I told them the secret story.

David calls on me now and then. He's suspicious at first, but then he transforms into my father, and we talk about the deep caverns of earth.

Someday soon I will join Wheeler in the search for undiscovered deposits of God. And late at night, he will transform into my father and we'll laugh at the good times that never fade away.

About the Author

Walter Mosley is the author of numerous bestselling works of fiction and nonfiction, including the acclaimed Easy Rawlins series of mysteries. The first Easy Rawlins novel, *Devil in a Blue Dress*, was made into a feature film starring Denzel Washington and Don Cheadle. Another work, *Always Outnumbered, Always Outgunned*, for which Mosley received the Anisfield-Wolf Book Award, was made into an HBO feature film starring Laurence Fishburne. His science fiction books include *Blue Light*, *Futureland*, and a bestselling novel for young readers, *47*. Born in Los Angeles, he has been a potter, a computer programmer, and a poet. He lives in New York.